Time

Guardians:

The Centaur's Curse

Also by Gareth Baker

Rogue Racer

Time Guardians:
The Minotaur's Eclipse
&
The Mini Missions

Brackenbelly
and the
Beast of Hogg-Bottom Farm

Brackenbelly
and the
Dragon Duct Forest

Moggy on a Mission

Star Friend

The Night I Helped Santa

Super Rabbit

Coming soon
Brackenbelly
and the
Village of Enigmas

Time

Guardians:

The Centaur's Curse

Gareth Baker

First published by Taralyn Books in February 2019

Cover art from TheCoverCollection.com

Formatting by Locutions Press: www.locutions.co.uk

Edited by C Tomkins

ISBN : 9781795030366

For the real Lola.

Guardian and Equipment Profiles

Theo Harpe

Age: 12

The youngest ever member of the Guardians of The Net. As the 100th person in the bloodline of Theseus, he is the Kyrios ton Pithon, which means Lord of the Vases in Greek. Theo can communicate with the spirits of the old heroes and borrow their skills and abilities to help him complete his dangerous and vital missions.

Xever Harpe AKA Pappou

Age: 63

Theo's Cypriot grandfather, who lives in Cyprus. He is the 98th Guardian and protects the Hall of Heroes. His daughter (Theo's mother), never became a Guardian. Pappou has secretly been training Theo to become a Guardian since he was very young by telling him Greek myths, teaching him to scuba dive and many other useful skills. Theo and Pappou have always been close but they grew even closer after Theo's grandmother and father died.

The Hall of Heroes

The secret base of the Guardians, the Hall of Heroes is a cave hidden away in a secret location known only to the current Guardians. This hideaway is the home of two very important things. First is Oracle, the living spirit of The Oracle, an ancient fortune teller capable of seeing the future. She has access to all knowledge known to humanity and the gods. Second is the collection of ancient vases which hold the spirits of the ancient heroes.

The Sword of Chronos

Created by the gods, this weapon is not only super-light and super-sharp, it allows Guardians to create portals so they can travel through time and space. It is also used to send escaped beasts back to the Net. The Net is an energy field created by the gods to imprison the ancient beasts.

The Medallion of Morpheus

This gift gives a Guardian the ability to look like anyone he or she wishes. There are rumours that it is capable of much more, but that knowledge has been lost in the mists of time.

The Mirror of Aphrodite

Used by Guardians to communicate with each other or Oracle. The signal can travel through time as well as space.

CHAPTER ONE

Theo thought fighting the minotaur had been exhausting, but so was climbing a steep, rocky footpath in the Lake District.

How did I end up here? he thought, as he grabbed the rickety safety rail that was the only thing stopping him falling down to a rushing river three metres below.

The answer was simple. Last year, he and his mum, who was a famous archaeologist, had gone to Cyprus for the summer. This year, she was staying at home to conduct research at the university, meaning Theo would be at home for the whole six weeks being looked after by his grandparents. So he wouldn't get bored, and he wasn't a burden on her in-laws, she decided to book him on a five-day activity break.

After the adventures of last summer, Theo wasn't sure how the activities listed on the program would compare in terms of thrills or 'coolness', as Mum had assured him they would be. But the worst part was staying in a holiday cottage with people he didn't know.

When they arrived in a clapped-out minibus, Theo was pleased to find they each had their own room. The three youth workers who were with them, Daniel, Amanda and Hector, helped them to unload and told them they could choose any room they liked, as long as they made good choices.

Theo chose a room next to two of the seven other children. He knew Faroq and Mia from school. Faroq was the Year 7 football star. Mia had only just started Manor Park Comprehensive just before the summer holiday, but she had already gained a reputation.

She liked to be different and wanted everyone else to know. Her hair was long and dark, apart from the left-hand side and the back, where it had been cropped to a grade two. While everyone else was wearing walking gear and waterproofs, Mia was wearing Doctor Marten boots with tartan trousers. She wore a pink top with a unicorn on it. The mythological creature was sticking its tongue out and farting rainbows. Around her wrist, she wore a chunky gold bracelet.

The other five kids came from schools on the other side of town and the only one Theo had got to know on the minibus was Lola. She was nine and talked about unicorns the whole way. Mia got annoyed, but Theo liked her energy and enthusiasm.

After unpacking and a quick meal, they began the

walk. They had been following the snake-like path for what felt like hours. It slowly grew steeper and steeper as it climbed beside a fast-flowing river that wound its way down the forested hillside.

'What's that noise?' Mia said.

'It's a waterfall,' Amanda answered. 'It's what we've come to see.'

'Nice,' Lola said. 'I've never seen a real one.'

'Is it big?' asked Faroq.

'You'll find out in about two minutes,' Daniel said. 'It's not far, but the climbing gets a bit harder around this next bend.'

They followed the unevenly stepped path around an enormous boulder that seemed to grow out of the ground like the head of a buried giant.

'Wow!' Lola cried, stopping in the middle of the path.

In front of them was a stony beach-like area and beyond that a towering waterfall that dropped into a large plunge pool. The noise was incredible, a mixed up, chaotic sound that also seemed strangely rhythmic and planned at the same time. To the left of the waterfall were more steps, presumably leading to the top of the waterfall. Next to them was a pile of tree trunks that had been cut down. Theo could see the stumps which had been left in the ground.

Theo stood next to Lola. She turned and smiled up at him before looking back at the waterfall.

'Isn't it beautiful? I bet unicorns live behind it,' she

said. 'Look, there's a shelf of rock that goes behind the water.'

'Maybe,' Theo answered, not wanting to get dragged into another unicorn discussion.

'See how the water sparkles? That's unicorn magic.'

Theo smiled kindly.

'Right,' said Daniel getting a camera out of his backpack. 'Let's get a group photo and carry on.'

'Say "waterfall",' Amanda chirped, as Hector took the picture.

Theo put on a cheesy grin and glanced across at Mia, who was making ears behind Lola's head with her fingers.

'Come on then, gang. Time to get moving,' Daniel said, swinging his backpack back on and heading to the next set of steps. They had been purposefully constructed and were much wider than the previous ones, which had been mostly made from the rocks in the ground. Here, three or four people could walk together at a time, and they had been built out of gravel and huge pieces of wood, like railway sleepers.

Theo smiled when he saw over the top of the steps and the land beyond. They were at the top. His initial sense of excitement quickly disappeared. The land, while flat, went on and on until it met snow-covered mountains in the far-off distance.

'Snow?' said Faroq. 'It's the middle of summer! What's going on?'

'It's cold up there,' Amanda said. 'Don't worry, we'll be okay. We're not going up that high.'

'I'm not worried,' Faroq muttered. 'Hey, what's that?'

One hundred metres away, something sat in the middle of the track, almost covering the width of its stony surface.

They were half-way towards whatever it was, when Lola said, 'I think it's a quad bike.'

'Cool!' Faroq and Mia both said. They started running. The other children quickly followed.

'Keep away, everybody,' called Daniel.

When Theo caught up, everyone was studying it. He, however, looked out across the fields around them. There was no else around. How had the vehicle got there?

He turned back to the group just as Mia jumped onto the saddle and started making the sounds of an engine revving and tyres skidding.

'Mia—' Daniel began.

'Get off that — now!' shouted an angry voice, cutting Daniel off.

The man appeared as if out of nowhere. Judging by the clothes he was wearing, he was a farm worker. He had something large and dirty-white balanced across his shoulders behind his head.

'Oh my...' Lola said, disgust clear on her face as she pointed at the man. 'Is that what I think it is?'

'I don't think it's a unicorn, no,' said Mia.

'I said, move it,' said the farmer, pushing his way through the crowd to the back of the bike.

Mia jumped off just as the farmer grabbed the hooved legs that hung down on either side of his head and dumped the load he was carrying onto the back of the quad. He reached into his torn jacket pocket and pulled out a tangled mess of orange twine.

'It's a sheep,' Faroq said, looking a bit confused.

'Well done, Sherlock,' said Mia, peering closer. 'Is it...dead?'

'Afraid so,' the shepherd answered as he started to tie the poor animal down.

'Come on, everybody,' Daniel said, ushering Theo and the others along. 'Let's leave this gentleman to it.'

'I wouldn't go that way if I were you,' the shepherd called. 'There's danger out there.'

CHAPTER TWO

Everyone stopped walking and Theo felt Lola's hand brush against his. He didn't have the heart to ignore her, so he took hold of it.

'Why's it dangerous?' Daniel asked.

'Look at those clouds. Snow's on the way.'

'It's the middle of the summer. It's not going to—'

'It's been threatening it for days,' the shepherd continued. 'Ever since that strange electrical storm we had.'

'Snow wasn't on the weather forecast,' Hector said.

'We have our own weather around here. It's the mountains,' the shepherd said, pointing. 'They do strange things to the air and clouds. But, it has been worse the last few days. Really uppity.'

'Thanks for the warning, but we'll take our chances,' Daniel said.

'I really wouldn't. The snow's not the only danger.'

'What else is there?' Daniel said. Theo could hear the frustration in his voice.

'This sheep. It's not the first time one's just dropped dead for no reason. There's something out there in the hills. Loads have gone missing over the last few days. Since the storm, actually.'

Lola squeezed Theo's hand.

'What kind of something?' Mia said, sounding more interested than afraid.

'A giant. There's been stories for years — hundreds of years — but yesterday I saw some footprints and—'

'Come on, everyone,' said Daniel, glaring at the shepherd. 'It's just a local legend. He's just trying to spook you all. It's nothing. Come on.'

Everyone began walking, but Theo couldn't help but look back over his shoulder and watch the shepherd finish tying the sheep to his quad.

'Why don't we sing a song?' Lola said. Everyone groaned, but Amanda and Hector started singing a very annoying song about a baby shark. Soon everyone joined in. Even Mia.

As they walked away from the shepherd and his dire warning, the air grew steadily colder. Twenty minutes later, just as the shepherd had predicted, white flakes began to drift down from the sky in thick clumps, grabbing at Theo's clothes and settling on the grass on either side of the track.

'I love snow,' said Lola, running into it, her arms wide like she was trying to hug it.

'Me too,' answered Theo, trying to sound cheerful.

Inside, he was worried. He'd only seen snow a few times in his life, and most of those had been in foreign countries, but he couldn't remember it falling this thick and fast, even in Norway, when Mum had been looking at Viking remains.

'Daniel, I think we should turn back,' Amanda said, coming to a halt.

Daniel stopped and nodded. 'I think you're right.'

'No way. I was really enjoying being out in the cold with feet that I can't feel any more,' Faroq said, with obvious sarcasm. 'Do we have to?'

'We'll be okay, won't we Amanda?' Lola asked.

'We'll be fine,' Theo said, crossing over to her. 'Don't worry. We'll soon be back home in the warm. It's all downhill. It won't take as long to get back as it did to get here.'

'Theo's right,' Amanda said, giving Theo a 'thank you' smile. 'Once we're back under the trees, they'll shelter us from the snow. Hector, you take the lead.'

Everyone turned round and began walking back towards the waterfall. The track soon began to disappear under the snow as it dropped thicker and faster.

Theo tucked his hands up into his sleeves and wondered how much further they had to go before they got back to the waterfall. Perhaps the shepherd would come back for them with a tractor and trailer.

'What's that sound?' Faroq said, stopping in the middle of the snow-covered track.

Theo squinted and brushed snow out of his eyebrows. There was something ahead in the middle of the track under the rapidly growing blanket of snow. It sounded like...an engine.

Theo felt the hairs on the back of his neck stand on end. Something was wrong. It was the quad, and it was tipped on its side. The sheep was no longer tied on the back. And the shepherd was nowhere to be seen. He couldn't explain why, but something didn't feel right. And it wasn't just the upturned vehicle and the missing shepherd. Snow in July? They were in the Lake District, true, but they weren't high in the mountains.

'Come on, leave it alone,' Daniel said.

'But why's the engine still running?' Lola asked.

Good question, Theo thought.

He felt a familiar stirring inside him. It was the heroes. Danger must be close by if they were awakening. He wasn't worried though, their presence always filled him with a sense of calm. They guided him, helped him and warned him of danger. He had learned to trust them implicitly over the last year.

'Let's not worry about that. We need to get to shelter. Come on, everyone,' Daniel said. 'Let's speed up a bit, Hector.'

They began to move off except for Theo. The thickening snow away from the track had grabbed his attention. There was something odd about it. Walking through the crisp whiteness, he ignored the cold dampness that started to spread through the bottoms of his hiking trousers.

'What's this?' Theo said to himself, as he looked at the shape in the snow.

Look more closely, Theo, said a voice inside his head in heavily-accented English. It had been a while since Theo had heard his ancestor inside his mind, but he knew it was always a good idea to listen to Theseus.

'Theo, come back!'

Theo barely heard Daniel's voice as he crouched down, his shaking fingers reaching out to the strange indentation in the snow.

'It's a footprint,' Theo said, his words disappearing in a cloud of hot breath. 'But it's almost as big as me.'

He stepped away. Was the shepherd's story true? Was there a giant? Anyone else would have dismissed it, but not Theo. He'd fought the minotaur, seen harpies and talked to Zeus, king of the gods.

'Theo?' Dan shouted from behind him, his voice snappy.

'Just give me a minute,' Theo said, his eyes sweeping across the white blanket. There were more footprints. They were so wide apart, Theo thought he could probably fit a small car between each one.

'We need to go. Now,' Daniel shouted.

'I said, give me a minute,' Theo replied.

'Move it,' Daniel said, with a jerk of his head. 'And don't ever speak to me like that again.'

'I'm sorry, Daniel. But I think we're in terrible danger.'

'Well spotted, Theo,' Daniel said. 'Come on, we

need to catch up with the others before this snow gets so thick we can't see our hands in front of our faces.'

'I don't mean the snow. Look!' Theo pointed, first in front of him and then at each footprint as he half-ran, half-jumped over the snow from one to the next.

Theo thought he saw Daniel roll his eyes as he came closer.

'What am I supposed to be seeing?' Daniel asked, putting his hands on his hips.

'Look. There's a footprint. A huge one.'

Daniel shook his head. 'Theo, that man's story about giants? He was just trying to scare you.'

'It *is* a footprint. Look again. And why would the shepherd just leave his quad bike tipped up on its side?'

'He skidded in the snow and it turned over?'

'But why leave it there?'

'Maybe he wasn't strong enough to turn it back over.'

'So where has he gone? Why take the dead sheep? And why leave the engine running? And how do you explain these footprints?'

'It's just an optical illusion. A pattern in the grass under the snow,' Daniel said, taking a deep breath. 'Come on, we're getting left behind, and I've a hot drink with my name on it back at the cottage.'

Theo ignored him and stepped through the snow towards the next footprint.

'Theo, come on, or I'll leave you.'

Theo ignored the leader's threat — he knew Daniel

would never do it. His eyes flicked to the next print. And the next. Something terrible dawned on him. The footprints were heading towards the waterfall.

Theo ran awkwardly through the snow, towards the others, towards the waterfall. His heart raced. He no longer felt cold when he skidded to a halt at the top of the stairs that led down to the plunge pool.

From below, a roar of anger drowned out the constant drone of the waterfall. Theo swallowed. Whatever had made it was large.

'What was that?' Daniel shouted, his voice a little high-pitched, as he waddled up the path, catching up and trying not to slip over.

'Trouble. *Big* trouble.' Theo took off his backpack, his numb fingers fumbling with the straps.

'What do you mean? Big trouble?' Daniel asked, stopping and bending over to get his breath back.

'Stand up straight,' Theo said.

'Why?'

'So you can hold this.' Theo thrust the backpack against Daniel's chest, who grabbed it in shock. Theo tugged open the zip. He reached inside the bag and threw away the jumper he'd been told to bring.

'You might need that!' Daniel protested.

'That's not going to help us right now. This will.' Theo stepped away from Daniel, gripping something in his hand.

'What's that?'

'No time to explain,' Theo said. He felt the comforting movement of the metal hilt of the Sword of

Chronos as it shifted and moulded to fit his grip perfectly. A gift from the gods and crafted by the great god Hephaestus, the sword held incredible secrets and powers, including time travel.

'What the...' Daniel gasped as a blade appeared out of the hilt in Theo's hand.

Theo turned towards the steps. If the footprint belonged to what he thought it did, the others were in danger. Only one type of giant loved sheep, and it wasn't renowned for its intelligence.

Theo started down the wide staircase towards the plunge pool, the steps almost invisible under the trampled snow. Luckily a wooden safety rail was there to guide him.

'Theseus, are you still there?' he said.

We're here, said a new voice inside his head. *We're all here.*

It was Odysseus. Theo had never heard his voice before, but somehow he knew who it was.

Although they were inside his mind, the heroes were three thousand miles away, their spirits hidden in ancient vases in the Hall of Heroes. Theo should have guessed Odysseus would come and help him. The great hero and his crew had escaped from a cyclops thousands of years ago, blinding the giant in the process.

Theo thought he was about halfway down the steps when the snow swirled furiously in the air, making it even harder to see. From out of the whiteness below him, four of the children he was on the camp with came hurtling towards him. They ran straight past him, their eyes filled with terror.

One stopped and grabbed Theo's arm. 'We need to get away. There's a thing… a huge—'

The frightened boy didn't finish his sentence. The ground shook beneath their feet and he fell up the steps. Theo toppled against the wooden safety rail.

'It's…it's coming,' the boy said, getting back to his feet.

A deep roar came from below, hidden within the whiteness. Suddenly, the snow rushed towards them and a huge, indistinct shape appeared from further down the steps.

'Keep going,' Theo said.

'What about you?'

'I'll be fine,' he replied.

Theo was in his element here. He felt confident the heroes and his equipment would help him to defeat the beast. He just had to make sure everyone was safe. 'Where's Lola and the others?'

'I don't know. We saw…we saw this…this thing and everyone scattered.'

Another roar filled the air.

'Daniel's at the top of the stairs. Quick, go,' Theo said, walking down the steps. The ground shook every few seconds and then the beast appeared from out of the snow, his feet mangling the steps beneath them.

First, Theo saw its head as it came up the stairs and drew level with him. Then it rose higher and higher as the thing continued, all the while revealing more and more of itself. When it stopped, its feet were still a whole flight of stairs below Theo.

Theo stared up into the beast's singular eye. That settled it. It was definitely a cyclops. Its head was bald, except for a few wisps of hair blowing wildly in the air. His skin had the red glow of coldness about it and apart from a ragged sheepskin wrapped around his waist, it was naked.

It's Akanthus, cousin of Polyphemus, Odysseus said.

'Polyphemus, the cyclops you blinded?' Theo said, remembering the story that Pappou had taught him years and years ago as part of his secret training.

Yes. If I'd known we would be here thousands of years later, I might have chosen another strategy to escape his cave, said Odysseus sarcastically.

'Akanthus,' Theo called. 'Surrender and I will return you to the Net unharmed.'

The cyclops looked confused, let out a deep roar and raised his arm, ready to smash it down.

Theo quickly lunged forward with the sword.

Panicking, Akanthus threw himself back from the end of the glowing blade. His eye widened in surprise for a moment and then he toppled backwards.

Theo watched as the cyclops disappeared back into the tumbling snow. The ground shook with the impact of the great beast falling down each and every step.

Now he would be *really* angry and Lola and the others were down there with him.

CHAPTER THREE

Theo slowed as he neared the bottom of the stairs. It hadn't been easy coming down them. Almost every step had been smashed by Akanthus's falling body.

At the bottom, a hole marked where the cyclops had finally landed. The snow and stones had been forced deep into the ground, revealing the soil beneath. Theo hoped none of the others had been around when the beast had landed. The stones would have formed deadly missiles as they scattered everywhere.

Uneven footprints led away from the hole, following the edge of the pool towards the stairs that entered the forest and went towards the holiday home.

Theo surveyed the area around the plunge pool. It wasn't easy to see anything. The air around him was a curious mixture of falling snow and water vapour that rose from the plunge pool like a cloud of steam.

Stepping around the ragged indention, Theo followed the footprints along the edge of the water until they went no further. Where had Akanthus gone? Down the stairs? Had he seen the others and—

A roar came from his Theo's right.

Move!

Theo immediately obeyed Odysseus's command and went into a forward roll, the snow crunching beneath him.

A huge boulder crashed onto the ground where he had been moments before, sending up a shower of rocks and snow. It bounced back up and plummeting into the pool, sending water in every direction.

'Thanks, guys,' Theo said.

Crump, crump, crump, crump!

A dark shape came out of the snow and mist. Akanthus must have doubled back to the stairs he'd fallen down and waited in ambush. Theo cursed himself for not thinking to check there.

The cyclops rushed closer carrying something in his hands. Something large and dangerous-looking. Theo raised his sword and bent his knees, ready to act.

With a deep roar, Akanthus fully emerged from the swirling snow, brandishing a tree trunk. One end had been cut off by a chainsaw. The other was thick with roots like he had ripped it out of the ground.

The giant took a wild swing with his improvised

club. Theo jumped back to avoid it. Some of the roots whipped past, dangerously close, stinging his cheek.

Theo braced himself for the next attack, but Akanthus staggered past him, the power of his swing taking him off balance. His enormous feet stumbled into the edge of the plunge pool. He wobbled precariously as he fought to get his balance, then he dropped down as his leg disappeared into the chilling depths.

Theo looked at the sword in his hand. What good would it be against a weapon that was almost as thick as his own body?

Don't worry about that. Stay focused. Seek solutions, not problems, said Odysseus.

Akanthus stumbled from side to side, struggling to get back out of the water. For a moment, the beast's eye grew wide and confused, then he fell backwards with an enormous splash.

You see, said Odysseus. *Akanthus' lack of intelligence is your best weapon. Use it! But be warned, he will grow angrier the more frustrated he gets.*

Theo backed away from the edge of the pool. The distance would give him the time to think and come up with a cunning plan.

Maybe he could set up his own ambush?

Theo ran towards the stairs that headed down towards the cottage. As soon as he left the beach and entered the forest, the snow and steam cleared. He ducked around the first of the many zig-zagging corners and threw his back against the giant boulder he'd gone around earlier.

Once he was sure he was out of Akanthus' sight, he unzipped his waterproof coat and reached inside. He pulled out the bronze medallion that hung around his neck. He looked at the face on it. The first time he'd seen it he'd thought it was Albert Einstein. In fact, it was Morpheus, the god of dreams. Just like the Sword of Chronos, it had power.

And he had an idea for how to use it.

Stuffing the medallion back down his T-shirt, Theo zipped up his coat. It was time to get back up to the top before Akanthus found the others.

Theo activated the medallion and stepped around the boulder.

A high-pitched scream split the air.

Theo looked up and found Lola standing at the top of the stairs in front of him. Her mouth was open even though her scream had ended. Behind her, Mia was also staring, open-mouthed.

'It's only me,' Theo said, but it was too late.

The medallion could make him look like anyone he wanted. And he'd asked it to make him look like a cyclops.

'R...r...run,' Mia managed to say, as she grabbed Lola's hand and dragged her away from the stairs.

Back towards Akanthus.

'Stop, stop,' Theo cried.

Leaving the medallion activated, Theo took the first step after them. His feet felt leaden, his whole body seemed to move much slower than usual, like he was feeling stiff after a cross-county run. He didn't *feel* tired *or* stiff though. Something was different about the way the medallion was working, he was sure of it.

He rounded a corner and the wooden safety rail at the edge of the path leant to the side and snapped.

'What…?' Theo said, looking at its ragged edge. 'How did that break? It moved all by itself!'

I'm not quite sure, but I think you *did it. It seems the medallion is affecting the environment around you.*

'Odysseus, you sound like Oracle. What do you mean?' asked Theo, confused.

That's because I'm talking to her. She says that the medallion is creating an aura around you and that it is no longer simply affecting people's minds.

'An aura? What, like a bubble? A ghost?'

Yes, something like that. Oracle isn't sure, but she hypothesises that somehow the medallion is creating the form of a cyclops around you.

'So, I'm actually becoming one, not just messing with people's heads?'

You are not actually turning into one, but—

'Do I have the strength of one?' Theo interrupted.

I don't know. No Guardian has ever used the medallion to be anything other than a human before.

'I think it's time we found out,' Theo said and stomped up the last of the steps and out of the trees.

CHAPTER FOUR

Theo stepped back onto the snow-covered, beach-like area by the plunge pool. He instantly spotted a huge, dark bulk through the mixture of steam and snow.

Akanthus. It had to be.

He rushed closer to Akanthus, his legs sluggish, and came to an abrupt halt, skidding in the snow. What he was looking at couldn't have been any worse. The indistinct shape in the snow had become clearer. It *was* Akanthus.

But it was also Lola.

The cyclops loomed over her, his hand reaching down to lift her off the ground. Or worse.

'Akanthus, it's me, Polyphemus, your cousin,' Theo called, stepping closer. Despite the heavy atmosphere and the roar of the waterfall, Theo heard his own words — deep and guttural — echo around the hard walls of rock that surrounded the plunge pool.

Akanthus froze, his hand in mid-grasp around Lola's body. 'Cousin?' he said, surprise clear in his voice.

'Let the puny human go,' Theo said, moving closer still.

Akanthus didn't reply. Instead he picked Lola up and lifted her into the air. Her legs kicked wildly as he brought her up to his one eye and sniffed her with his wide, flat nose.

'I smell your fear, human,' said Akanthus. 'Good. It make you more tasty to eat.'

Theo tried to swallow, but his mouth had gone dry. He was confident he could look after himself, but now Lola was in danger and that wasn't something he was prepared for.

'Put her down, cousin. Let us feast on sheep,' Theo said, thinking quickly. 'I can smell them, taste them. My stomach yearns for them. It has been too long, trapped in that terrible void.'

'You want me to let her go?' Akanthus said, scratching his bald head with his free hand.

'Yes,' Theo replied. 'If we eat her, more humans will come. Humans with weapons.'

'If...if you say so, cousin. I hadn't thought of that. You were always the clever one.'

Theo held his breath as Akanthus lowered Lola down to the ground. As soon as Akanthus moved his hand out of the way, Theo called, 'Run, girl.'

Lola turned and ran. Amanda appeared from out of the thick atmosphere and grabbed her hand. Together they disappeared, hopefully to find the others.

Theo was about to turn his attention back to Akanthus when Mia appeared.

'You guys are amazing,' she said, showing no fear as she came closer. She looked up at them both and then suddenly Mia's gaze dropped until Theo was sure she was staring straight into his *real* eyes.

Theo was just about to roar at her to leave when she gave a crooked smile, turned and disappeared into the snow towards the stairs.

Theo looked over at Akanthus and gave a huge sigh of relief.

'Polyphemus?' Akanthus said, as he walked over to him. 'Me can't believe you let them go. You *hate* humans.'

'But I *love* sheep,' he replied, patting his tummy.

Akanthus laughed. It was a deep and filled with real joy. 'How Me have missed you, cousin.'

Without warning, Akanthus threw his arms wide and went to wrap them about his cousin. Theo panicked. Akanthus was so tall — Theo could have walked between his legs — his arms would meet nothing and the illusion would be ruined.

Theo looked up, waiting for the inevitable, when he saw something amazing. There was a ghost-like image of a cyclops' body, arms and head above him and Akanthus' arms were wrapped around it like it was solid.

Moving his real arms, Theo watched in amazement as the huge, translucent ones far above him wrapped around Akanthus. 'Wow,' he whispered. Even though he wasn't actually touching Akanthus, he could *feel* the cyclops' cold body on his own skin.

Oracle was right, Theo thought to the heroes. *The medallion is creating a physical form around me. This is amazing!*

'Me have cave,' Akanthus said, looking at the waterfall. 'It's behind there. It is cold and dark, and the sound of water drives me mad, but it was all Me could find.'

'Me would love to see it, but Me must go,' Theo said, glancing at the waterfall.

'Aw, come on, cousin. It this way,' said Akanthus. Before Theo could say another word, the cyclops was off. He walked into the water. It rose up past his knees and then up to his middle.

Theo stopped at the water's edge. There was no way he could walk into the water. He would end up underwater even if the projection that had formed around him wouldn't. He wasn't inside it after all.

'Come, cousin, what keeping you?' Akanthus called. He stood in front of the waterfall, the fierce torrent of water splashing off his broad shoulders like it was nothing other than a power shower.

'Me have changed my mind,' Theo said looking down at the swirling water and the bits of wood and litter that were caught in the current in the centre of the plunge pool. It looked cold and uninviting. 'You were right. Me want to go after the humans. You stay here and get the fire ready.'

'There is no need. Me already have a nice warm fire inside, and enough sheep for a banquet. Me even have a human. He was with metal horse. I'm sure he make a nice treat for you.'

Theo felt his shoulders slump. Akanthus must be talking about the shepherd. He couldn't leave the man there. Now he *had* to go with Akanthus.

Bracing himself, Theo stepped into the bitterly cold water. He took another step and stumbled just as Akanthus had a few minutes earlier. It was so cold — so impossibly cold — Theo found it difficult to breathe. He stopped, unsure he could take another step. His whole body shook violently and he knew he couldn't face submerging his shoulders. And if his head went under water...

If only he was *inside* the projection, maybe it would protect him just as it had stopped Akanthus' hugging arms.

Theo stopped and looked at Akanthus. The cyclops climbed up through the cascading water and disappeared through it.

Theo glanced at the beach. Now that Akanthus could no longer see him, perhaps he could leave the water and try to make his way down the shelf of rock?

Keep going, said Theseus. *You're almost there. You have made it through the worst of it.*

Theo knew the hero was right. He walked on. The freezing water slipped over his shoulders, taking his breath away. Spray from the waterfall hit his face, drenching his hair.

That was it, he could go no further without putting his head under water.

Perhaps you could swim, Theseus suggested.

Theo was about to reply when his foot slipped out from under him, rolling on pebbles at the bottom of the pool. The cold water rushed up over his lips and nose before he went under completely. He thrashed about in panic, forgetting all the swimming and diving skills Pappou had taught him.

Stand up!

The voice cut through his fear, and without realising, he did what he had been commanded to. He felt his feet touch the river bed. Theo tipped his head back and lifted his mouth out of the water and started to breathe again.

Just as he was getting his breath back, he felt his feet leave the riverbed. He felt the chilling water roll off his shoulders and he rose out of the water, like he was standing on a platform that was slowly rising up.

Odysseus, what's happening? Theo thought.

I don't know. This is new, too. It must be the medallion.

Theo looked at the projection around him. He was now at the top so that his arms were inside Polyphemus's. But there was more. Theo knitted his eyebrows together and stared at what was happening around him. The projection was becoming opaque, more solid, as if he was now inside a large rubber suit.

Maybe it was because I wished I was inside the projection, Theo suggested.

That is certainly a possibility, Theseus replied.

Tentatively, Theo took a step forward.

Just move and act. I think the medallion will do the rest. It's trying to make things easier for you.

Theo nodded, his tongue poking out in concentration as he walked forward, trying to ignore the fact he was *on* the water. His huge cyclops form waded through the water until it reached the waterfall. The water bounced off its shoulders, its power threatening to force him back under water.

Oracle says to not think about yourself and your own limitations. You are Polyphemus, the cyclops. You do have a giant's strength, said Odysseus.

Theo reached forward and his projected hand gripped the rock shelf on the other side of the water. He hauled himself up and disappeared through it.

Theo's eyes widened in amazement. In front of him was a cave mouth, not quite tall enough for his taller cyclops-self to walk down. Stalactites hung from the top, looking like teeth ready to devour any who entered.

Theo stepped inside, water draining from his clothes. His whole body shook with the cold, but mercifully the air inside the tunnel was quite warm. Theo looked at the projection around him and smiled in amazement. It was shaking too!

'Come on, cousin. My stomach is rumbling,' Akanthus called from somewhere ahead.

Theo moved down the passage, bending slightly to avoid banging his head on the stalactites. He glanced at the floor six or so feet below him. It was a bad choice. It made his head spin and his stomach churn.

Let the medallion do the hard work for you, said Odysseus. *Trust it the way you trust us.*

Theo nodded and started walking again, dodging the stalactites.

Ahead, flickering orange light reflected off the walls of the cave, reminding him of the Hall of Heroes. As he turned the corner, he found Akanthus next to a large fire. No wonder the air was warmer in here. The fire was huge, like a bonfire on November the fifth. Parts of the floor were covered in more of the stone, teeth-like structures, only this time they grew up. Theo was pretty sure they were called stalagmites. Nearby, the shepherd was tied to one, his head slumped to one side.

Theo looked across at Akanthus. He had a burning log in his hand.

'Is something wrong, cousin?' Theo asked.

'Yes. You are.'

'Why? What do you mean?'

'For a blind cyclops, you found your way in here very easily.'

'I followed your voice and—'

'Enough of your lies. Me not stupid. Me can see your eye.'

'My eye,' Theo said, reaching up to touch his forehead.

'Yes, Me think it is very well-healed.'

Theo lowered his hand. When he'd imagined himself as a cyclops, he hadn't thought about the ancient injury Odysseus had given Polyphemus.

And now his one mistake had revealed who he was.

CHAPTER FIVE

Theo deactivated the Medallion of Morpheus. The semi-solid projection around him instantly disappeared and he dropped two metres down to the floor, bending his knees to absorb the impact. As he stood back up, he extended the sword of Chronos again.

'You're right, I'm not Polyphemus.'

'A boy?!' Akanthus said, tipping his head to one side.

'Not just any boy. I'm Theo, a Time Guardian, a descendant of Theseus, a Guardian of the Net.' He paused and pointed the blade at Akanthus. 'And I'm here to send you back to where you belong.'

'Now it all make sense,' Akanthus said, scratching his bald head again. Despite his words, he really didn't sound like it made any sense to him at all. 'Now Me see why you let humans go. You...you tricked me. Me will defeat you and add you to feast instead,' he said, his tone angry, his voice louder.

'You can try,' Theo said, and reactivated the Medallion of Morpheus with a single thought. First the translucent field formed around him — the wide, muscular legs, the rotund body, arms with fists as big as school desks — and then Theo felt his feet leave the floor. He wobbled as he rose up, but even though he tried to relax, it felt wrong to have no control over his own body. Just as his shoulders were in line with Akanthus's, he came to a halt. Once again, he was stood inside the torso of the great beast.

Theo's confidence grew. Even looking down at the ground didn't faze him anymore. It was like his body and the projection were one. The heroes were helping him.

Akanthus let out a roar that made the forest of stalactites vibrate above them.

And charged.

Theo dived to the right to avoid the wild swing of the burning log. He hit the ground and rolled between two stalagmites.

Or he *should* have done.

His body was small enough to go between them. His projected shoulders were not. The pillars of rock shattered, sending shards of rock flying in every direction.

Theo cried out in pain. He grabbed at his right shoulder. It throbbed and felt sticky. But when he looked, there was nothing there. He glanced at the same place on the projection. Through the translucent body, he saw blood running down the arm from a nasty-looking wound.

Oracle doesn't think you will suffer any injuries, but you will get tired, and if the projection is beaten, it will cease to exist and you will be unable to create another for a while, said Theseus.

'Good to know,' Theo said, a groan of pain escaping his lips.

No more time to explain. Get up, he's coming.

Akanthus swung the burning log up over his shoulder and ran through the fragments of stalagmites towards Theo.

It was already too late for him to get up. Theo had to defend himself as best he could from where he lay. He brought the Sword of Chronos up. It looked tiny in his outstretched hand, but further out, Theo saw the much larger form, grasped in his translucent arm.

Theo braced himself for the impact as the two weapons connected. Vibrations ran down his arm, but he *was* strong enough to resist the blow. Akanthus's weapon hovered a metre or so above his body, blocked by the larger version of the Sword of Chronos.

'Me will kill you, boy!' Akanthus roared, spittle flying from his mouth as he pressed down with the burning log, forcing both the real and the projected sword back down towards Theo.

'I can do it,' Theo said to himself. 'I have the strength of a cyclops.'

He drew back his foot and kicked out. His larger

foot slammed into Akanthus' knee. The cyclops staggered back.

Now, get up! Odysseus cried. *You're an easy target on the floor.*

Theo looked at the ground, which was a metre below him, the projection's huge, flabby back between him and it. He rolled over to get on one knee.

'Woah!' he cried as his stomach lurched like he was on a rollercoaster. He was thrown up into the air as his giant knee levered him up. Feeling dizzy, Theo reached out to steady himself and his projected hand slapped down onto the floor.

Stop thinking about it! Odysseus hissed. *See what you want to happen in your mind and...*

'I get it!' Theo shouted before muttering to himself, 'I think.'

Akanthus came at him again, angrier than before. Theo watched the incoming weapon, imagined blocking it, and brought up his own weapon.

The two weapons collided, the sword slicing a huge chuck out of the Akanthus's wooden weapon.

'You hurt my little stick!' Akanthus roared, swinging at him again. Theo brought the sword up, trusting the medallion to work. Its super-light, super-sharp blade sliced straight through the burning log, sending the flaming end spinning off into the darkness of the cave, narrowly missing the farmer.

Akanthus looked down at the wooden stump in his hand, dropped it on the floor and stamped on it like an angry child. 'Now look what you made Me do,' Akanthus said, pointing at the remains of his weapon.

'You don't belong here, Akanthus. You need to go back to the Net.'

'Never,' Akanthus roared. 'Me like it here. There's sheep. And light, even if it is cold. Me won't go. Me hates it there. Hates it. Me crush you!'

Akanthus moved his arm back to take another swing, stopped and looked at his empty hand. A small, disappointed groan escaped his lips.

'Give up, Akanthus,' Theo said, smiling triumphantly.

'Me punch you. Me—' The giant stopped as his eye fell on the ceiling. A deep chuckle erupted from his mouth. 'Me no punch, Me skewer!'

Theo stepped back as Akanthus reached up, wrapped his huge fingers around a stalactite and ripped it off the ceiling.

'Now you scared,' Akanthus laughed before throwing his improvised javelin.

Theo ran towards the exit, his own legs slow, moving at the same speed as the huge ones that stomped beneath him. He heard the missile shatter on the ground behind him. Bits of stone flicked up and hit his fleeing legs. He felt the usual pain but didn't dare look at the damage to the projection.

He glanced back at the cyclops. The beast already had a second stalactite in his hand and was preparing to launch it. Theo needed to send Akanthus back to the Net, soon. There was only one problem. How could he make a portal large enough to send him back? And even though Akanthus wasn't that clever, even he would see a crackling, humming rip in time and space.

You'll think of a way, Theseus said inside his mind. *You have to.*

Akanthus threw the stalactite and immediately reached up for another.

Theo flung himself at the cave wall next to the tunnel entrance and turned to face Akanthus just in time to dodge the weapon.

And the next.

Theo looked down the tunnel at the cascade of water at the other end.

'Akanthus, if you want me, you'll have to come and get me,' he shouted. He pushed himself off the wall and ran down the tunnel towards the waterfall, dodging the stalactites as he went.

'Come back, boy,' Akanthus roared.

Theo glanced over his shoulder. The cyclops was lumbering after him.

Half-way down the tunnel, Theo deactivating the medallion and dropped down to the ground, returning to his true self.

He ran towards the water. Saying the secret incantation that would activate the sword in his head, Theo watched the Sword of Chronos begin to glow a bright, brilliant green. Now it was no longer just a sword.

Now it could make a portal to any time and place Theo could picture.

'You will not escape me, boy!' thundered Akanthus, as he entered the tunnel. He rushed forward, his shoulders smashing through the stalactites, either too stupid to dodge them or too desperate to catch Theo.

Theo didn't look back. Instead, he jumped off the ledge, up into the air and through the freezing water. As he burst out the other side, he twisted his body around to face the wall of water and brought the sword up above his head.

As he began to drop towards the plunge pool, he swung the blade down. Its glimmering edge cut through the air, splitting it like an open wound. Its edges sparked and hissed as he dragged the blade down through the air, making the portal as long as possible.

When he felt the ice-cold grip of the water around his legs, Theo shut off the blade and held his breath. Thrusting his arms out, he slowed his descent through the water and then began to kick.

Theo's face broke the surface. Before he could take a lungful of air, the curtain of water burst outward in a great wave. Akanthus emerged, his legs still moving in a running motion, a fierce bellow drowning out even the sound of the waterfall.

There was just enough time for Theo to see the beast's reaction as it disappeared through the portal.

Turning himself back into Polyphemus, Theo swam towards the waterfall and climbed up into the hidden cave tunnel. It was time to check on the shepherd, then he could get out of here.

Returning back to normal, Theo tucked the sword hilt into his sodden pocket and ran down the tunnel.

'Help! Over here,' the shepherd cried. 'Get me out of here.'

'It's all right,' Theo said. 'He's gone.'

'No, no. There were two of them. They were fighting. If they come back— Wait, it's you, from that group of kids. You're all in danger. Quick, let's get out of here.'

'They're gone,' Theo said. 'You're safe now. Everyone's safe.'

'Really?'

'Really.'

'Oh wow,' said the shepherd. 'I told you, didn't I?'

'Told me what?'

'That the stories of the giant were real. This…this is going to make me rich. Rich beyond my wildest dreams,' the shepherd said.

'Oh no,' said Theo, getting up and stumbling away. 'What have I done?'

'Saved my life, that's what. But don't worry, I won't keep all the money to myself. I'll give you, what? Five percent.'

Theo turned his back on the shepherd and began to walk away. He'd got so excited he hadn't thought about the consequences of what he was doing. Being a Guardian wasn't just about putting escaped beasts back in the Net. It was about keeping it all a secret.

People had seen him. And the cyclops. Now what was he going to do? He looked down at the sword hilt in his hand and had his second great idea of the day. All he had to do was travel back in time and change it all before any of it even happened in the first place.

CHAPTER SIX

Theo stepped through the portal and into his bedroom at home. He ran straight to the door and frantically felt along the top of its frame, searching for the key to his desk.

He'd already made one big mistake by exposing his secret.

And then his clever plan to go back in time and cover it all up had only made it worse.

Hands trembling, he found the key, slid it into the lock of his desk drawer and turned it. Yanking the drawer open, he lifted the false bottom he had made from a piece of laminate flooring he'd got from his English grandfather and removed the folded pillowcase that was hidden beneath it.

Theo stopped and stared at the bundle in his hand for a moment before unfolding the fabric, reaching inside and withdrawing the gleaming object that was hidden within.

It was a hand mirror, cast from solid bronze, its face polished to a super-smooth, reflective finish. The handle was fashioned into the figure of the goddess of love and beauty herself. In fact, it had once belonged to her.

Just like the sword and medallion, it had been created by the Greek gods thousands of years ago. Unlike the sword and medallion, he'd decided to leave the Mirror of Aphrodite at home. Theo regretted the choice now. If he'd taken it, then maybe things wouldn't have gone so horribly wrong.

Theo stared at the mirror and tried to calm himself down while he took a moment to decide what he was going to say to Pappou. Adjusting his fingers so they lay in the right places to make it activate, Theo braced himself for delivering the bad news.

He gazed into the polished surface and waited for the old man's face to appear. Hopefully his grandfather would have his usual friendly smile and one of his bright Hawaiian shirts on.

'Pappou, are you there?' Theo said, trying to keep the panic out of his voice. If he explained what had happened, carefully and rationally, he was sure Pappou would see he was only trying to sort things out.

Theo waited and waited. Perhaps he was holding the mirror wrong. He checked the position of his hand. Everything was right. What was taking his grandfather so long?

'Theo,' came Pappou's voice eventually, his accent

a mix of English and Greek Cypriot. 'I had a feeling you'd be calling. I've just arrived at the Hall. Oracle's going wild. What's happening?'

Theo swallowed. Of course, *she* would know everything. 'I'm sorry, Pappou, I've...I've made a terrible mistake.'

'Tell me,' Pappou said, his face slowly appearing in the mirror as the connection between it and the one Pappou held grew stronger. Theo looked at his grandfather's smile. He was a very patient man. Hopefully patient enough for the welcoming expression to stay.

'I'm coming to you. I need...' Theo paused while he thought of the best word to use. 'I need your advice.'

'By the tone of One Hundred's voice,' came a woman's voice, 'I would assume he is anxious. And if the temporal readings I am getting are correct, I can see why.' It was Oracle. The words she chose had a habit of making her sound like a computer, but she wasn't. Theo wasn't quite sure what she was.

Pappou reappeared in the mirror. 'What's wrong, Theo?'

'It will be better if I tell you to your face. I'm coming. See you soon.'

Theo dropped the mirror on the bed, severing the contact, and sat with his head in his hands, hoping that Oracle didn't tell Pappou before he got there. He gathered a few things, including the mirror, and put them into his school bag, took a deep breath, opened another portal to the beautiful island of Cyprus, and vanished.

Pappou was pacing around the Hall of Heroes in his wetsuit when Theo arrived. Since Theo had taken possession of the Sword of Chronos, his grandfather had to swim into the Hall of Heroes via the secret underwater tunnel. Theo was glad he didn't have to do that anymore. While he was an excellent scuba diver, travelling through the tight passageway that first time was more than enough.

'What in Tartarus has happened?' Pappou said, moving towards Theo as he emerged from the crackling portal.

Theo walked past the white marble table that was made in the style of a Greek temple, straight over to the chest that contained a collection of special clothes and sat down on it. Theo filled his grandfather in on everything that had happened with the cyclops.

Pappou was about to speak when Theo hung his head and said, 'I'm afraid there's more.'

'Go on,' Pappou said, patiently.

Theo looked back up at his grandfather. His face looked warm and welcoming, but there was concern in his eyes. Theo also thought he looked tired, his skin drawn and thin.

'I tried to fix it. I tried to make it right, so they couldn't tell anyone about what they saw.' Theo paused and ran his hand through his hair. 'But…but I made it worse.'

'What did you do, Theo?' Pappou asked, placing his hand on his grandson's shoulder.

'I thought if none of it ever happened, it would be okay. So I made a portal and travelled back to the cave an hour earlier.' Theo stopped.

'Go on,' Pappou urged.

'I am finally making sense of these readings,' Oracle said. 'I can explain if it makes it easier for you, One Hundred.'

'No!' Theo said, a little louder than he intended. 'This is my mess, I must clean it up. I…I just might need your help.'

'So, you went back in time and what, sent Akanthus back into the Net?'

'Yes. He was fast asleep. He hadn't captured the shepherd yet. I had timed it perfectly. I opened a portal and tricked Akanthus into waking up and falling through it. I celebrated, Pappou, I actually celebrated because I thought I had managed to stop it all from happening. But then…'

'What happened next?' Pappou said, sitting next to Theo on the chest, placing his hands on his knees as he lowered himself down.

'Instead of making another portal to leave, I walked out of the cave. There was this hidden shelf of rock behind the water and I really wanted to walk along it. It looked really cool, and…' Theo looked away from his grandfather. 'And when I came out from behind the water, I saw a group of people having a photo taken.'

'And they saw you?' Pappou said. 'That's not so bad.'

'No, Pappou. You don't understand. *I* was in the group. It was me and this group of kids that Mum sent me away with. Pappou, what have I done? There are now two of me! I tried to make a portal to travel through time so there wouldn't be two of us but...' Theo stopped.

'But it would not work?' said Oracle.

'No.'

'You are not allowed to use the sword to change your own history.'

Theo looked at Pappou, unsure what the old man would do next. Suddenly his whole body went cold as he thought of something. 'Which...which one of us is the real me?'

Pappou smiled. 'You are, of course. Try not to worry.'

'Try not to worry?' Theo cried, running his hand through his hair. How could Pappou be so calm about it all?

'Theo, you acted quickly and decisively, and that's important,' Pappou said. 'You have carried out the duties of a Guardian of the Net and returned the beast to the place where it rightfully belongs, and more importantly, protected the people of Earth.'

'Yes, but it's even worse than I realised. I thought I'd just given away our secret, but now I've created another me and I can no longer use this to carry out my duties.' Theo reached inside his pocket and pulled out the sword hilt.

'You have created what is called a time paradox,' said Oracle. 'It has the potential to cause time and space to completely unravel and therefore everything to cease to exis—'

'Not now, Oracle,' Pappou snapped, a little too late.

'The whole world could end?' Theo asked. 'Because of me?'

'Not just the world, the whole uni—'

'Oracle, *will* you shut up,' Pappou hissed.

'Yes, Ninety-Eight.'

'So how do we put it right? How do I get rid of the second version of myself? How do we make the sword work again? How do we stop everything from…?' Theo was close to tears.

'We'll think of a way, Theo. I promise,' Pappou said, taking him in his arms.

Theo couldn't remember the last time he'd had a hug. It was probably at his father's funeral. The memory of that sad day was the final straw and Theo began to cry, his whole body shaking. Any secret hopes he still had of using the sword to bring his father back were now utterly destroyed.

Grandfather and grandson stayed like that for a few minutes. Even Oracle stayed quiet. Finally, Theo separated himself from his grandfather, turned away and wiped his tear-streaked face.

'Oracle?' Pappou said, pushing himself off the chest with an audible groan.

'Yes, Ninety-Eight,' she answered. 'Am I permitted to talk now?'

'Now isn't the time to argue,' Pappou said, as he slowly made his way to the table. 'I think we have no choice but to call upon His Majesty.'

'Are you sure that is wise, Ninety-Eight? The amount of power that I have to draw upon to make that possible is—'

'There *is* no other way.' Pappou turned and looked at Theo. 'Come and stand beside me.'

Reluctantly, Theo did as he was told. It was as they bumped shoulders that he noticed that he was almost as tall as his grandfather. He had grown, he knew that, but Pappou's shoulders looked slumped and his back arched, making him appear shorter than he was.

'Are you all right?' Pappou asked.

'Yes,' Theo lied, thinking *When did Pappou get so old?*

'Don't worry, Theo. I'm sure Zeus will be...helpful. You weren't given the full training of a Guardian and were rushed into action. Had you received the full instruction like me, you would have known this would happen.'

'Ninety-Eight, I have managed to raise His Majesty,' Oracle said, a second before the space between the table and its roof began to sparkle with lights. The tiny particles came together and formed into the shape of Zeus's head. Theo had spoken to the king of the gods before, but power had been so low that his face hadn't formed and they had only heard his voice. He looked exactly the way he imagined — all beard, long hair and muscles.

'Xever, Kyrios ton Pithon,' Zeus said, his deep voice booming out from his long, white beard.

'My Lord,' Pappou said, getting down on one knee. Theo quickly copied his grandfather.

'Rise, my faithful servants,' said Zeus.

Theo got up and waited for Pappou, who gripped the edge of the table with one hand and pushed down on his knee with the other so he could get back up.

'My Lord. We have a situation,' Pappou said.

'I am aware of the creatures escaping from the Net. Kyrios ton Pithon, you must put a stop to that,' Zeus said, using Theo's official title — The Lord of the Vases.

'He will, My Lord, but there is another issue that we need your help with. I ask you to listen and remember that Theo has not had all the necessary training.'

'I grow tired, Xever. What is this "issue"?'

'In his inexperience, Theo — I mean Kyrios ton Pithon — has created a time paradox, and—'

'And what Xever? You want me to put it right?' Before Pappou could respond, the old god continued. 'Of course. It is not, after all, the first time that the boy has done this. But, it *will* be the last. You had better ensure that Kyrios ton Pithon receives the appropriate training. Fixing these mistakes takes up the

Pantheon's energy and...and I have a feeling that our enemy is going to make a move again. And soon.'

'Of course, My Lord.'

'Kyrios ton Pithon?' Zeus said.

'Yes,' Theo answered, adding 'My Lord' after receiving a jab in the ribs from Pappou's elbow.

'Return to the Lake District and go to bed. When you wake up, everything will be as it should. Now, go, put it right and return here as soon as you are able. Xever, it is time you told him the truth and completed his training.'

The hologram winked out and the Hall grew darker.

'Told me the truth? What did he mean by that?' Theo asked.

Pappou smiled. 'It can wait. I promise. Now, since you can't travel through time at the moment, it looks like you'll have to stay here with me until it's the right time in England for you to return to. What shall we do? Scuba diving? Parasailing? Or would you like to go to the taverna?'

Theo smiled for the first time in an hour and knew everything, at least with his grandfather, was going to be all right.

CHAPTER SEVEN

In the end, Theo and Pappou settled on going diving. They stayed out, enjoying the warm water, until it was almost dark. By nine o'clock, Theo was exhausted and he went to the bedroom Pappou kept for him. He found sleeping impossible. His mind was just too full — Pappou looking old, the end of the world (again) and having to let the dreams of saving his dad go, once and for all.

Two hours later, Theo got back up, having not slept a wink, and re-joined his grandfather. They ate halloumi and olives in the living room until Pappou fell asleep, a glass of Zivania in his hand.

Finally, it was late enough in Cyprus to be the right time back home. Theo covered his grandfather with a blanket, kissed him on the head and whispered good-bye. Then, taking the Sword of Chronos in his hand, he created the portal that would take him back to the Lake District and stepped through.

Theo thought his heart stopped beating when he found his other self lying in the bed, fast asleep. He stepped closer. It felt strange looking down at his doppelganger. It looked small and vulnerable. Theo hadn't been sure what he thought would happen when Zeus told him to go to sleep, but it wasn't this.

Unsure where to wait, or even what he was waiting for, Theo sat down on the floor, leaned against the wall and watched the body sleeping in his bed.

And watched.

His eyelids began to droop. He tried to hold them open, desperate to know what would happen, but it became too difficult, like something other than tiredness was compelling him to sleep.

It was beginning to get light outside when Theo awoke. He glanced at the bed. It was empty, the quilt ruffled but not thrown back as he always did when he got out of it. It was as if the other Theo had simply disappeared from beneath the covers.

He got up and was about to climb into bed when something occurred to him. What had happened to his twin? Was he somewhere else? Or had he simply ceased to exist? Had they somehow become one again? What, if any of this, would he remember when he woke up again?

It was all too much to think about. Theo climbed

into the empty bed. It still felt warm. Theo shut his eyes once again.

Hours later, Theo was awoken by a loud hammering on the door.

'Theo, let me in.'

It was Lola.

'Sure…okay,' Theo called back, still half-asleep. He felt thick-headed. He'd had some really strange dreams in the night about cyclopses and shepherds. And he had the left-over taste of olives in his mouth. He must have forgotten to clean his teeth before he went to bed. But after they had come back from that boring walk into the hills, Daniel and Hector had cooked them pizza for tea. As far as Theo could remember, none of them had olives on.

'Theo?' Lola called again.

'Yes. Come in.'

The bedroom door flew open and Lola came crashing in.

'Come on, you're late. Faroq's been knocking on your door for ages. We're off to some caves today.'

'Great,' Theo said, 'not more caves.'

'What do you mean? Don't you like caves?'

'No. It's just…'

'Just what?' Lola asked.

Theo rubbed his head. Didn't he go to some caves yesterday? Wasn't there a…

'Are you all right?' Lola asked, stepping closer.

'Yeah,' answered Theo, rubbing his temple. 'It's nothing. I had some weird dreams last night, that's all. They seemed so real. But now I can't remember them. And the more I think about them, the foggier they get.'

'That's normal. Happens to me all the time. Come on!' Lola said, grabbing Theo's hand. 'I've been sent up to tell you that you have ten minutes and then we're going without you.'

'I'll be right with you.'

'Good. Don't be long,' Lola said, slamming the door behind her.

To Theo's surprise, the caves turned out to be really cool, even if the stalactite the owners were so proud of turned out to be tiny compared to how the photo on their leaflet made it appear.

The rest of the camp flew by.

On the third day they went to Bowness and visited the Beatrix Potter (or Pooter as Faroq insisted on calling her) World. Lola loved the models of the animals. She eventually found them more interesting than Theo and stopped following him everywhere.

On the fourth day, they went to an adventure park. First, they climbed through an aerial obstacle course that made its way through the branches of trees and ended with a zip-line.

Hector got stuck halfway down so Lola refused to have her go.

In the afternoon, they learned how to make fires and Theo was forced to work with Mia because no one else would. They lit their fire the quickest, and as a reward were given marshmallows to cook.

That night everyone sat in the shared area in the holiday home playing Cluedo. They all began yawning, but they refused to go to bed. Tomorrow was the last day and most of it was going to be taken up with driving back home.

The minibus drive home seemed to take forever and despite being exhausted, Theo couldn't fall asleep, no matter how hard he tried. Eventually, the minibus pulled up outside his house. At least he was going to be the first one to get dropped off. Theo looked out the window and watched his front door open. He suddenly realised he'd missed his mum and he couldn't wait to see her.

His heart sank when his grandmother and grandfather stepped out of the front door. The sense of disappointment was quickly replaced with regret. His dad's parents were great, even if it was in a different way to Pappou. It wasn't their fault Mum wasn't at home and they had been drafted in to look after him.

'See you at school next week,' Mia said, as Theo gathered all his stuff. 'It's been cool to get to know you. I know we didn't get off to a good start. I…I find it hard to get to know people.'

'It's okay,' he replied. 'I wasn't keen on going on

the holiday and meeting new people either, but it was fun.'

'Yes, it was,' she agreed. 'Want to meet by the school gates at 8:30 on the first day back?'

'Erm,' Theo said, a little surprised at her request. 'Yeah, sure.'

'Hey, everyone,' shouted Faroq. 'Theo's got a girlfriend.'

'Get lost, loser,' Mia said, throwing a stray sock she found on the floor at him. 'Would you like my phone number?'

'Erm, I..' Theo said. He really wasn't sure if he did want it, but he found himself digging his phone out of his pocket anyway. Before he had a chance to stop her, Mia grabbed it out of his hand and started swiping and tapping the screen.

'There you go, I've done it for you.'

'Thanks,' Theo said, as he shrugged his backpack on and grabbed his daypack. He thanked Daniel and Amanda as he climbed out and went over to his grandparents. He turned back to the minibus and felt his gran put her arm around him. Faroq smiled mockingly out the window. Mia smiled too. It made her look completely different.

The minibus started up again, belching out a black cloud from its exhaust, and pulled away. Everyone inside waved or pulled faces. Lola looked across at Mia. She didn't look very happy with her. Suddenly Theo felt bad for ignoring Lola for the last couple of days, but she had teamed up with the two other girls on the camp.

'Did you have a nice time?' Gran said, with a welcoming smile.

'Yes, thank you. Where's Mum?' he asked, already knowing the answer.

'She had to stay late at the university,' Granddad said, 'so she asked us to pop by so someone would be here to meet you.'

Theo nodded and made a smile that didn't go all the way up to his eyes.

'Why don't I make you a nice cold drink and a sandwich?' Gran said.

'Did I ever tell you about the time your dad went camping with his friends?' Granddad said, taking the backpack from Theo and leading the way up the footpath.

'Yes,' said Theo. 'But I'd love to hear it again.'

CHAPTER EIGHT

Theo laughed at his granddad's story, even though he knew what was going to happen. It had taken Theo a long time to listen to stories about his father without getting upset. He knew his grandfather used to find them hard to tell, too. His son, Theo's father, had died while riding a motorcycle in Cyprus when they had been on holiday visiting Pappou.

'Mum's texted,' Gran said, popping her head around the door. 'She's on her way home and she's asked me to put some dinner on. Any requests?'

'Can we get fish and chips?' Theo said. 'Dad loved fish and chips.'

'Yes. Yes, he did,' said Granddad. 'Come on, let's walk to the chippy, I could do with stretching my legs.'

'How was your trip?' Mum asked, as she pushed a green chip to the edge of her plate and searched for another that was more to her liking.

The four of them sat around the dinner table, the smell of batter, chips and vinegar strong in the air.

'It was pretty cool. We went to a cave,' Theo said.

'Your dad loved caves,' Gran said.

'What did you learn?' Mum asked. Theo thought she asked the question far too quickly, probably trying to avoid the subject of his father. As usual.

'I learnt how to make a fire with Mia,' Theo said with a smile.

'Did you learn anything useful?' Mum asked, looking across at him.

Theo felt the joy of the memory drain from him. As far as Mum was concerned, if it wasn't something academic, it wasn't worth learning.

'I'm tired,' Theo said, pushing his plate away and standing up.

'But you've hardly eaten a thing,' Gran said. Theo noticed her subtle glance at her daughter-in-law. 'Besides, I want to hear more about this Mia.'

Theo felt his cheeks go warm.

'Was that the girl you were talking to on the bus? The one who had a weird haircut?' said Granddad.

'It's not weird. I think it looks quite cool,' Theo said.

Gran and Granddad smiled at each other.

'I didn't mean it like that,' Theo stammered.

'Why? What did you mean?' said Gran.

'Who *is* this girl?' asked Mum. It was clear that her interest was not the same as her parents-in-law. Knowing Mum, she would want to know all about Mia's family and make sure that she was a suitable friend who would not get Theo into trouble.

Theo smiled as he imagined the mischief the pair of them could get into. Maybe he should become friends with her, just to annoy his mother. He ignored the question and went round to the other side of the table.

'Night, Gran, Granddad,' Theo said, kissing them both on the cheek. Granddad grabbed him, placed his fist on the top of his head and rubbed his knuckles across his hair. Theo struggled just enough to play along. He knew he could easily break out of his grandfather's grip if he tried to, but it was something they'd done for as long as he could remember.

'We'll see you soon,' Granddad said. 'You can tell us all about your fire.'

Theo's smile returned briefly. 'I'd like that. Night, Mum,' he said, leaving the room.

He was just about to shut the door when he heard Gran say, 'Elizabeth, you're too hard on that boy.'

Theo wasn't sure if he was pleased Gran was sticking up for him or not. He went to the bathroom, cleaned his teeth and then climbed into bed. Despite the curtains, the room was still too light to sleep.

Not that he intended to.

He just needed to get away. Ever since Dad died, Mum had just been...so serious. Maybe she'd always been like that and he was just too young to remember. Or maybe Dad, who had been so fun-loving and crazy, just brought out the fun in her. Theo knew she missed him, of course she did, so did he, but they still had each other. Maybe both Mum and Mia acted the way they did to hide their true feelings and fears. But if Mum couldn't talk to him, who could she talk to?

Theo turned and looked at his holiday luggage. Granddad had brought it upstairs for him and then Gran had emptied all the clothes out and took them back downstairs to be washed.

He was about to open his daypack and remove the god-powered artefacts when he noticed the small, blue light on his phone was flashing. He'd left it in his bedroom to charge because Mum insisted there should be no phones or tablets at the table. He swiped his thumb across the screen.

It was a message from Mia.

Thanks for a cool few days

Theo lay in bed not sure how to answer it. He never texted anyone apart from his mum, and besides, Mia was a girl. That could make things very awkward.

A soft *ding* rang out and another message appeared.

It was good to get to know you. It's been weird not really knowing anyone.

Theo assumed she was talking about school. His thumb moved across the screen and wrote, ***No problem.***

Phew! I thought you were ignoring me lol.

Theo stared at his screen, unsure how to respond to her comment, he simply put, ***Wish I was still away.***

Theo put his phone down and turned his attention back to the pack. He unzipped it and removed the sword and mirror. The medallion, as usual, was around his neck, under his t-shirt. He moved to his desk and was about to place the Mirror of Aphrodite back in its hidden compartment when he had a strange feeling. He was sure he hadn't taken the mirror with him on the holiday. He shrugged his shoulders. He must have changed his mind and forgotten. How else would the mirror end up in his pack?

Gripping the mirror in the special way, he gave Pappou a call.

There was no answer.

His phone *dinged* instead. Theo picked it up and smiled at the two devices he held, one ancient and one modern. One made by the gods and one by man.

What are you up to tomorrow?

He answered, telling Mia that he didn't know and that he'd let her know later. Right now, he had other questions he needed answering, and there was only one place to find them.

Theo put the mirror back in the pillowcase and hid it under the false bottom in his drawer. Then he picked up the sword hilt from his bed and crossed to his bedroom door to make sure no one was coming up the stairs. Once he knew it was safe, he summoned the blade and opened a portal to the Hall of Heroes.

The Hall was in darkness. Theo put the hilt of the sword in his pocket and snapped his fingers. The torches on the cave walls flickered to life, one at a time. Their faint green light reflected off the pale surface of the smooth walls. He walked up to the temple table and rested his hand on the red fabric. Underneath it were the slots to hold the sword and the mirror.

'Oracle,' he said. 'I need some answers.'

'Of course, One Hundred. I knew you were coming as soon as you activated the portal,' came her disembodied voice.

'Then why didn't you turn the lights on for me?'

'We must *all* save energy.'

'True,' Theo said, remembering the power drain from last year. Hadn't Pappou mentioned something about power when he came here asking for help?

Theo shook his head. Again he had that strange feeling that something had happened, that he had a memory, but when he tried to focus on it, it just disappeared.

'How can I help you, One Hundred?'

'For a start, can you please call me Theo.'

'I will try, Theo. Your grandfather has also insisted I call him by his given name. It is a challenge, especially when the numbering system works so well.'

'I'm more than a number, Oracle.'

'I am sorry, Theo, I did not mean to imply you were nothing more than a mathematical construct. When you have been alive as long as I have, there are an awful lot of names to remember.'

'You're alive?' Theo asked.

'I...I exist, but not in a corporeal form.'

'A what?'

'A corporeal form. A body. It comes from the Latin word corpus, which means body.'

'Like a corpse,' Theo said, feeling proud that he'd worked it out.

'Exactly, One Hundred.'

'So,' Theo said, ignoring Oracle's slip, 'how do you exist?'

'Like the heroes in the jars and the sailor you met out in the ocean last summer, I am alive in the form of my essence. Instead of a jar for my home, I inhabit this cave.'

Theo looked across at the shelves of vases. The first time he'd seen them, he'd been amazed. One moment there was a blank wall of pale stone, the next, shelves, carved into the rock, appeared filled with vases. Each was painted with the image of a person. Theo later learned each was a picture of the hero it contained.

'So, you're not *in* the temple,' Theo said, pointing at the beautifully crafted stone table in front of him.

'No, I am not. And that is not the temple at Delphi. It is a scale model of Olympus, with some minor alterations.'

'I had no idea,' Theo said, stepping back to admire it a little more closely. 'I thought I would be...larger. Posher.'

'Our High Lord Zeus and his family have everything they desire. What need of mortal things like riches and gold do they have? It is kings who seek to surround themselves with material possessions. I have noticed in this twenty-first century world that we live in, everyone seems to want to surround themselves with possessions. I remember the first time you came here you brought a tablet. Did you know—'

'Oracle?' Theo said, interrupting her before she could continue to lecture him.

'Yes, One Hundred?'

'I have some questions, remember?'

'I am sorry, One Hundred, you did say.' If Theo had upset her, she didn't show it. 'How can I be of assistance?'

'Well, this isn't what I wanted to ask, but since you just told me that's Olympus,' Theo said, pointing at the table. 'Where are we?'

'This is the Hall of Heroes. You know that.'

'Yes, but where is it?'

'Has Ninety-Eight not told you?'

'No, Xever hasn't,' Theo said, deliberately using Pappou's name.

'Where do you think we are?'

Theo smiled. He had given this question some thought and there really was only one possible answer.

'The first time I came here, Pappou and I sailed out to sea in his boat. Then I had to swim down that terrible tunnel. I'm fairly certain we were coming back to shore. Once you're in here, if you listen carefully...' Theo stopped and did just that. He had grown used to the sound now, but in the background, you could hear the sound of the sea. 'We're inside Aphrodite's Rock, aren't we?'

'Indeed, we are.'

It wasn't Oracle that answered. Theo turned at the sound of Pappou's voice. He was dressed in his diving gear, a scuba tank on his back and flippers dangling in his left hand. Theo rushed towards him, noticing his grandfather was moving slower than usual.

'Let me help you with that,' Theo said, grabbing the oxygen tank as Pappou slipped his arms free of its straps.

'Thank you,' Pappou said.

'Theo has come here in search of answers,' said Oracle.

'Good. There's something I've been meaning to tell him for some time.'

CHAPTER NINE

The smile on Theo's face instantly disappeared. He could tell by the tone of his grandfather's voice that whatever he had to tell him, it wasn't going to be good news.

'What is it?' Theo asked, dreading the answer. Was it related to how he was looking and acting? Was swimming to the Hall through the hidden entrance getting too much for him? Was he ill? Was...was he dying? Or worse — did he have Alzheimer's disease? Someone came into school to talk about it. Theo knew Pappou would hate to suffer from it. To lose all that he was, slowly, piece-by-piece.

'We really need to get some chairs in here,' Pappou said, leaning on the table.

Theo propped the oxygen tank against the wall and walked back to his grandfather.

'Ninety-Eigh—' Oracle began.

'Xever. My name is Xever,' Pappou said, with more than a hint of irritation.

'Why don't you sit on the chest,' Theo said, turning back to go and fetch it. Something was definitely wrong. Was Pappou in pain? Mum always said pain made people grumpy and short-tempered.

'Good idea, but don't move it, it's heavier than it looks,' Pappou answered. He made his way to the wall and sat on top of the chest, groaning as he bent his knees.

Theo waited for his grandfather to settle, took a deep breath and asked, 'What do you need to tell me?'

'Last year, when you put time back the way it was meant to be, we only achieved half of what we set out to do.'

'I know. Theseus still forgot to change his sails and his father still threw himself into the sea. You said there were some things we couldn't change.'

'All that is true, Theo. But that's not what I mean.' Pappou paused and Theo really began to fear what he was going to say. 'The thing is, we didn't get to the root of the problem.'

Theo's eyebrows knitted together. 'I don't understand.'

'The reason why the minotaur escaped from the Net in the first place.'

'You mean the rip? The rip in the Net?'

'Yes,' Pappou said, getting to his feet and walking back to the table.

'Well, that answers one of my questions,' Theo said, following him.

'Yes, you're right, that *is* how the cyclops escaped, assuming that was your question.'

'Cyclops? What cyclops?' Theo asked, confused.

Pappou paused for a little too long before saying, 'I must be getting confused. There have been so many recently.'

Theo nodded, accepting Pappou's explanation. 'And the gorgon from a few months back?'

'Exactly. And there was the cetus you came into contact with at the end of last summer, before you headed back to England. But that's not all. There have been a number of sightings of strange creatures reported on the internet. Unfortunately, we haven't been able to get any firm evidence as to whether they were an escaped beast or just a wild goose chase. People often like to fake things, just to become famous.'

'I know what you mean,' said Theo. 'There was a report on *Newsround*. Tales of a giant boar in the Spanish hills. A group of holidaymakers saw it when they were on a tour of a vineyard. And on *YouTube* a video went viral of a figure that was living in a forest in America. People thought it was Bigfoot.'

'Bigfoot?'

'Come on, Pappou, everyone's heard of Bigfoot.'

The old man shook his head.

'Bigfoot,' Oracle said, 'is a mythological creature that is supposed to reside in the Pacific Northwest of

America. Also known as the Sasquatch, or 'Wild Man', the first reported sightings were in the 1920s. However, before that, there were a whole host of local legends from the indigenous people.'

'And we all know mythological creatures are real,' Theo added. 'As you didn't get in touch, I assumed it was fake news and I wasn't needed, unlike the gorgon.'

'Right, let's assume they weren't fake sightings,' Pappou said.

'And other creatures have been escaping.'

'If that is the case, it means the rip is getting larger.'

'Or other rips are forming.'

'I hadn't thought of that. Well done.' Pappou reached out to put his hand on Theo's head. He stopped, but Theo took his hand and finished the movement. They shared a smile, and Pappou ruffled his hair. It was a sign of affection he'd always done, just as his other grandfather rubbed his head with the knuckles of his fist. 'I thought you were getting too old for that.'

Not sure what to say, Theo ignored the question and said, 'Oracle, these sightings we've been discussing, what order did they occur in?'

'I will need a moment to compile all the information. I cannot believe that I was unaware of some of it. It is...worrying.'

'Don't fret, Oracle,' said Pappou.

'Pappou is right,' Theo said. 'We need to move on and focus on the future.'

'Technically we need to focus on all time streams in order to complete our role effectively. And the future is not written yet, so we cannot monitor that, either.'

'I just meant... Don't worry about it,' Theo said, shaking his head. 'If more beasts escape, is there a way of tracking them once they're here on Earth?'

'I am already working on that,' Oracle answered. 'No more sightings will go by without me noticing, I can assure you of that.'

'I believe you,' Theo said, smiling at her haughty nature. Then a thought occurred to him. 'I have a question for you, Oracle. Why did it snow in the middle of the summer? Was it connected to Akanthus's escape?'

'I do not know what you are referring to.'

'Sorry, that was a dream I had. I keep getting confused. It seemed so real, sometimes it feels more like a half-forgotten memory rather than a dream.'

Pappou suddenly looked away and busied himself with adjusting the books that filled the columns on each corner of the table.

'What wrong?' Theo asked.

'Nothing,' Pappou replied.

'No. You're definitely acting weird. What's going on?'

'Perhaps we should just tell him, Xever.'

Now Theo was really worried. Oracle had used his grandfather's name.

'Oracle,' Pappou said, with a sigh. 'Tell him.'

'It is a memory,' Oracle said. 'You *did* encounter a cyclops while you were on holiday. His name was Akanthus. It got complicated and—'

Theo grabbed his head as a sharp pain speared through it. He gritted his teeth and tried to hold a strangled cry inside.

'Are you all right?' Pappou said, catching hold of Theo's arm.

'I'm fine. I'm—' Theo screamed, cutting off what he was saying. His legs buckled beneath him and he fell to the ground.

'Theo?' Pappou said, crouching down next to him.

Theo slowly removed his hands from his head and uncoiled himself from his foetal position. He blinked, and the pain eased away.

'Theo, are you all right?'

'I…I remember. Pappou, I have two sets of memories. There was a cyclops. What happened before and what happened after Zeus put it all right. I'd forgotten it all. But now it's back.'

'It would appear that both incidents are now compatible with your brain's chemistry,' explained Oracle. 'It must have something to do with the Hall. It may well be that you will forget again when you leave. It will make for an interesting study.'

'Not now, Oracle,' Pappou said, reaching out. 'Here, let me help you back up.'

Theo took his offered hand, but didn't put any of his weight on it as his grandfather pulled him up.

'It's best now that we move on. You know the truth. Just learn from the experience, all right?'

'Yes, Pappou.'

'Now,' continued Oracle, as if nothing had happened, 'to go back to your last question about the weather, from the data available, it would appear the mass of the cyclops was so large that the amount of energy it transferred from the Net to Earth was enough to somehow interfere with local weather patterns.'

'That sounds a bit vague, Oracle,' Theo asked, rubbing at his head. There was still a lingering bit of pain.

Pappou nudged him in the ribs. A sign that he shouldn't wind up the stuffy know-it-all. She might sound like a computer, but wasn't, and unlike a computer, she had feelings which, when upset, could result in sulks. Or worse.

'It is the best I can do with the data at my disposal,' she answered. 'I do, however, now have the other information that you requested. The Bigfoot in the hills, which was actually a satyr, was the first to escape. Next, it was the cetus, then the gorgon, the boar, and finally, the cyclops.'

'So the satyr has been here in our reality for some time. But why didn't you know? Oracle, how did that get past you? You *always* know.'

'I am at a loss for an answer, One-Hundred. As I have already said, it is troubling.'

'You look like you have something else on your mind, Theo?' Pappou said.

'I'm mostly trying to get to grips with all these new...old memories, but, what about the cetus that attacked me in the sea last summer? Don't you think it's weird it appeared at just the right time? It's as if someone released it just as I was about to get the vase we needed?' Theo glanced across at the shelves in the rock wall at the vase he had recovered from the seabed.

'You think someone is *letting* them out?' Pappou asked.

'Maybe not all of them, but it's possible, don't you think? Was the cyclops released into the Lake District because I was there?'

Pappou nodded, a look of deep concern across his face. 'It doesn't bear thinking about, but yes, I think you might be right. But who's doing it? And how do they know who and where you are?'

'Could it be the person who snatched Medea through the portal, just as we were about to capture her?' Theo suggested. He hadn't seen who was on the other side, but whomever he was had a chilling voice and commanded not only Medea but a host of harpies.

'The one she called Master?'

'Yes.'

Pappou rubbed his chin. 'That's certainly possible. We have been trying to find Medea, but she has disappeared from all Oracle's scans. But after the tricks she pulled last time, who knows if she's alive or not. Oracle?'

'Yes, Ninety-Eight?'

'I think we should put more of your resources into attempting to locate and track any more break-outs, don't you?'

'I am not sure I have the capacity to do that, what with our energy situation the way it is,' Oracle replied.

'Then shut down some of your other tasks.'

'Such as?'

Theo looked across at his grandfather. He was sure his face flashed red for a moment.

'The similar task you have running.'

'Are you referring to tracking the whereabouts of One Hundred?'

'Yes, Oracle,' Pappou said, his face growing redder.

'It's okay, Pappou,' Theo said, 'I know you just want to make sure I'm safe.'

'Exactly,' Pappou said, a little too quickly.

'So, what next?'

'I think we're going to need some help with this. It's about time you met some very good friends of mine.'

CHAPTER TEN

Theo stared through the portal Pappou had created with the Sword of Chronos. Apart from the location of the Net, which was already pre-programmed into the sword, the wielder of the sword needed to know where he was going in order to make the passage through time and space. Luckily, Oracle usually solved that problem for them.

'I'm going to get changed out of this wetsuit,' Pappou said, handing the weapon back. 'Don't go through without me. My friends can be a little nervous about unexpected visitors.'

Theo hardly heard his grandfather as he took in the wonders he saw through the buzzing opening. It was night on the other side, but about three hundred metres away, hidden at the bottom of a wooded valley between two mountain peaks, was a village lit up by flaming torches. A waterfall tumbled down the cliff on the far side of the valley. Considering Theo's recent experience with waterfalls, he liked the setting. It gave the whole valley a peaceful quality as the community sat there, snuggled on all sides by natural barriers.

The village was made of three circular streets, one inside the other, like the layers of an onion. Houses lay on either side of the roads and in the very centre of the village was a large, round market square with a roaring bonfire. Theo could make out people sitting around it, their bare chests reflecting the light of the flames. Most of the people had horses with them.

'Why's everyone got a horse?' Theo called to his grandfather.

'Look again,' Pappou replied.

Theo did as he was told and it dawned on him what he was really seeing. He'd seen one of these magnificent creatures before. It had been frozen in the form of a statue created by the deadly glare of a gorgon's eyes. Seeing one, a whole community, living and breathing, was a thing of beauty.

It wasn't a village of humans and horses, they were centaurs.

Theo knew that Pappou had only created a portal to travel through space, not time. That meant these centaurs were living on Earth at that very moment. How had they not been discovered by satellites? Or by the locals? And, more importantly, why weren't they in the Net?

'Oracle?' Theo called, tearing his eyes away from the amazing sight.

'Yes, One-Hundred?'

'How do they remain undiscovered?'

'Just as the Net was created to trap and hold the beasts, Zeus also created several places here on Earth where creatures who were capable of living in harmony with humans could stay.'

'I knew you'd be impressed,' Pappou said, reappearing in a pair of cargo shorts and one of his usual brightly-coloured Hawaiian shirts. 'Oracle, do we happen to have anything lying around that we can take as a gift. Had I known we'd be visiting, I would have brought something with me.'

'All you can see is all we have,' Oracle answered.

Theo looked around the cave. There was literally nothing they could part with. 'A gift?'

'In centaur society, it is very impolite to arrive without bearing some form of gift,' Oracle explained.

'What sort of gift would they like?'

'Well,' said Pappou, 'Centaurs love to party.'

Theo smiled, 'Actually I might have something, but I don't know how suitable it will be. Do they have electricity?'

'No,' Pappou said. 'Why, what's your idea?'

Theo reached into his pocket and pulled out his phone. 'This is full of music. You can't have a party without music. I'm due an upgrade soon. If I give it to them I can just download all my tunes again when I get my new phone.'

'I'm sure they'll love it, but how will you explain its disappearance to your mother?'

'I'm always losing it,' Theo said, shrugging his shoulders.

'Hmmmm,' Pappou said. Theo could tell his grandfather was a little uncomfortable with the idea. 'If you're sure you want to do it.'

'Yes, it'll be cool.' *Until the battery runs out,* he thought.

'Okay. We'd better get moving.'

'After you,' Theo said.

Pappou stepped through the portal. It snapped shut the moment Theo joined him on the other side. Theo shut off the blade and tucked the hilt of the Sword of Chronos in his pocket.

They found themselves on a path that wound its way down through the wooded hillside towards the centaur camp. Now, without the distortion of the portal, the village was easier to see. The buildings were simple, but solid, and expertly constructed out of wooden frames and stone, presumably from the forest and mountain around them. Perhaps the cliff wasn't natural and it was all that remained of the mountain they had taken the stone from.

'Right, let's take a steady stroll down to the village. No sudden noises or movement. Their scouts may well have already seen the portal, but they may attack first and ask questions later.'

'I thought you said they were your friends?'

'They are.'

'Halt! Don't move,' snapped a voice from the bushes on the left.

Pappou's arm shot out in front of Theo and forced him to stop.

'It is I, Xever, servant of our High Lord, Zeus, you can stand down,' Pappou called out to the thick wall of trees and bushes all around them.

A moment later a rustling came from either side of the track and two centaurs appeared. One pointed a bow at them, an arrow nocked and ready to fire. The other had a spear, thick and heavy-looking. It was more like a lance, Theo decided. The one carrying the spear trotted forward, its hooves ringing out on the stony path. He stopped, the point of his weapon mere centimetres from Pappou's chest. There was a moment of silence and then the centaur smiled and lifted the spear up, safely out of the way.

'Xever Harpe, you are welcome, as always. We heard someone coming and were worried the God Shield had been pierced. You have brought a friend, I see.'

'Klopian, this is my grandson, but I should probably introduce him to you with his proper title. This is Kyrios ton Pithon.'

Pappou had barely finished saying it when the centaurs lowered themselves down on their front legs, bowing, their human heads tucked in against their chest, arms by their sides, weapons on the ground.

Theo felt himself go red. Whatever he had been expecting, it hadn't been that. He looked at the pair of centaurs as they stared down at the ground in front of them.

'They're waiting for you to give them permission to rise,' Pappou whispered in his ear.

'Rise,' Theo said, remembering his conversation with Zeus. Thank goodness he had both sets of memories again. The two guards rose back onto all four hooves.

'You know the way, Xever,' Klopian said, and he retreated back into the bushes, taking up his sentry position once again.

Theo and Pappou continued down the path. Theo searched the bushes where the large half-horse-half-humans had disappeared but there was no sign of them. For creatures so large, they were exceptionally skilled at stealth and camouflage.

'I really wasn't expecting that reaction,' Theo said.

'The bowing? You'd better get used to it,' Pappou said. 'Though you will need to bow to Chiron.'

'Chiron?' Theo said in surprise, recognising the name from the stories Pappou had told him from the moment he was old enough to understand. '*The* Chiron? The centaur who trained Hercules and Achilles?'

'No, a distant relative though. He's just as wise and fierce, too. Don't worry, that's who we've come to meet. We go way back. I was probably only a little older than you are now when I first met him.'

The path led them out of the trees and they were on an open field that Theo hadn't been able to see through the portal. It must have been the angle he was looking at, he decided. There were archery targets and stuffed mannequins.

'As well as partying, the centaurs are accomplished warriors. This way,' Pappou said, crossing the grass and heading for the first curved line of buildings.

'How often do you come here?' Theo asked, as they walked between the outer layer of houses he'd seen from above. The streets were almost deserted. Flickering torches decorated the corners of each house, spreading a pool of light. Each house was different — patterns, colours, the way the stones were stacked or the wooden frame was built. The roads were cobbled like an old, Victorian street.

'I haven't been able to since you've had the Sword of Chronos.'

Theo wasn't sure, but he thought he heard a touch of sadness in Pappou's voice. He'd never really thought about how his grandfather's life had changed since he had become a Guardian — apart from all the extra swimming he'd had to do.

'We can keep the sword in the Hall, if you want,' Theo offered. 'Then you can use it whenever you want to. I don't want to stop you from seeing your friends.'

'No, *you* must have it, especially at the moment. Who knows when the next beast will escape and what chaos it will bring. We're almost there. I know this is all new and fascinating, but try not to stare.'

They passed through to the next street and the sounds coming from all the people gathered around the fire in the centre of the village grew louder. Theo could pick out laughter, singing and the sounds of unusual musical instruments. The glow from the bonfire's flames lit up the walls and gave the night sky a slight orange tinge.

'I think we'll avoid the centre for now,' said Pappou. He turned left and they followed the road, bypassing the fire and passing houses and shops, shut up for the night.

A female centaur, standing outside a house, nodded as they went past. Pappou returned the gesture.

They continued around the circle of houses until they were on the opposite side of the village, then took another road, straight through to the outer ring of streets towards the cliff and the tumbling waterfall.

They stopped outside a house that was far bigger than any of the others Theo had seen so far. The waterfall tumbled behind it, its water much less fierce than the one in the Lake District, it's sound almost melodic and calm.

Pappou walked up to the front door. It was much wider than a typical door, no doubt designed to allow the width of the horse's body through, and lit with lanterns rather than torches. The woodwork was decorated with swirling patterns, picked out by white paint that allowed the grain of the wood to show through.

Pappou knocked but there was no answer.

'He'll be out the back, practising,' Pappou said,

opening the front door and letting himself in. Theo followed him into a corridor and found another door in front of them.

'Won't he mind us just walking in?' Theo asked.

'We won't enter his house. This passage will take us to his personal training ground.'

Pappou turned right and walked down the passage. Theo couldn't see anyone ahead, but through the opening at the other end he saw a beautiful garden that stretched on until it met the cliff and waterfall. The plunge pool at the bottom of it formed a pond. A wooden bridge crossed over it. Around the water was an area of sand with stones forming patterns on top of it.

In the very centre of the garden was an archery target.

Theo looked closer at the target. Three quivering arrows, all in a tight group, were embedded right in the centre.

'Whoever shot those is good,' Theo commented to Pappou in hushed tones. 'Very good.'

'Hmmm,' Pappou replied. 'Yes, Theo. There's only one centaur that good, and it's who we've come to meet.'

CHAPTER ELEVEN

A centaur trotted into view, only this one was slightly different from the others Theo had seen so far.

Chiron's human half didn't stop at the waist. Instead of horses' legs at the front, he was entirely human with a horse's body and rear legs behind him.

His tunic was decorated with bronze swirls like the patterns around the front door. It covered his chest and came down to his knees. He wore leather boots on his human feet. A quiver of arrows was slung across his back. He held an ornately-carved bow, decorated with the same swirls.

'Xever.' His voice was deep, authoritative, but friendly.

'Your Majesty,' Pappou said, bowing. Theo quickly copied.

As Chiron came closer, Theo shuddered. The sound of his two hooves reminded him of the minotaur and the fear it had induced the first few times he'd heard them.

'And you must be Kyrios ton Pithon,' Chiron said to Theo, bending at the waist.

'I am, but you may call me Theo,' he said, trying his best to sound as important as his title.

'Whatever makes you happy, Theo.' He held out his hand and thrust it towards Pappou. 'Xever, my friend, what brings you here?'

'We come seeking your counsel and friendship,' Pappou answered, shaking his hand.

'That is already granted. I would ask if you have come to request training for the boy, but if he truly is Kyrios ton Pithon, he will need none.'

'He has shown remarkable skill and is learning every day, but one always requires training, great Chiron.'

'I see you still remember my first lesson, my friend.'

Pappou nodded. 'There are always new things to learn. Things about ourselves we can improve. But, Chiron, before we begin, may we present you with a gift.' Pappou turned to Theo, who reached into his pocket and stepped forward, revealing the phone.

'And what is this?' Chiron asked, as he ran his fingers over the smooth surface.

'It's a phone,' Theo answered, amazed there was anyone on Earth that didn't know that.

'Ah, I have heard of these, but never seen a real one. This is a mobile phone, correct?'

'Yes,' Theo answered, pleased Chiron seemed happy with it.

'And what need do I have of a mobile phone? Everyone I wish to speak to lives here with me. Present company excluded, of course,' he added, nodding at Pappou.

Theo felt a flash of sadness pass through him. At first he thought the feeling was because Chiron seemed to be rejecting his gift, but then he realised it was something else. He felt bad for the centaurs. While they were safe here, they were confined within this beautiful valley. As stunning as it was, it was a prison just like the Net.

Trying to keep upbeat, Theo said, 'I thought you might like the music on it. And, surely, the purpose of a gift is to express friendship, not to fulfil a need.'

'You make a very good point. Forgive my bluntness,' Chiron said as he began to swipe his thumb across the screen. A moment later, last week's number one came out of the speaker. Theo looked at his grandfather, surprised the centaur knew how to operate it. Theo heard a tapping sound and he looked down at Chiron's human foot. He was moving it in time with the music. His two rear hooves tapped out a different rhythm.

Chiron's laughter filled the air when the music went silent at the end of the song.

'This is wonderful. I will have to save it for special occasions so I don't drain the battery. Don't look so surprised, my boy. I have never seen or owned a mobile phone, but I have been schooled in their use. Now, Xever, why have you come?'

'It's bad news, I'm afraid. We don't have much time, and we are already on the back foot. The forces of darkness are moving once again,' Pappou said, killing the joyous mood.

'I fear you are right, my friend. We've been having problems of our own. Follow me, and I will tell you more.'

Chiron led them to the back of his house, past the sand garden and opened another decorated door.

'I'm afraid I have no chairs, Theo,' Chiron said, walking over to a large table in the centre of the room. Inside, the house was made up of one large living space. Apart from the table, and some wall decorations — pieces of natural art, weapons and brightly coloured wall-hangings — the only other thing in it appeared to be a walled-off section. Theo could see straw on the floor. Chiron's bedroom?

The centaur walked over to the wall of weapons and hung up his bow and quiver next to a lance-like spear, the pommel of which was decorated with the head of a hydra. He came back to the table where Pappou and Theo were waiting for him. While it was the perfect height for centaurs, its surface was just a little too high for humans to use. Theo felt like he was four again and trying to listen to Pappou and his parents as they sat around the kitchen table.

'You seem surprised at the lack of things in my house,' the centaur said to Theo. 'Unlike humans, we share everything we have. Right now, our market square has become a communal area where we all sit, eat and tell tales. You probably saw it when you arrived. You will come and join us?'

'I'd like that,' Theo said, wondering what a half-horse-half-human would eat.

'Good, we will do so later. Now, Xever, to business,' Chiron said, his tone turning serious. 'You said you had things to discuss.'

'Yes. Since the eclipse last year, beasts have been escaping from the Net.'

'That is not a surprise. When the minotaur damaged it, it was inevitable that others would follow.'

'I agree,' Pappou said. 'And at first we were able to track a handful of escapees, but recently...'

'There have been incidents you knew nothing about,' Chiron finished for him. He did not sound surprised. 'Tell me more.'

Pappou looked at Theo and gave him an encouraging look.

Theo cleared his throat and prepared himself. It was like doing show and tell at school, except it could be a disaster if he missed out a crucial detail. To make matters worse, what if he didn't know what the crucial information was?

'Erm…' Theo began. 'A cyclops escaped and ended up in England. It was pure luck I happened to be in the right place at the right time.'

Chiron smiled and put his hand on Theo's shoulder. 'I doubt it was luck, young man. The gods work in mysterious ways, and perhaps your own abilities, as well as the vases, somehow led you there that day.'

'Maybe,' Theo said, but he didn't believe it. His mother had booked him on the summer camp since he had brought home the advert at Easter. 'I was wondering if someone deliberately released it, knowing I was there.'

'If that is so, then that *is* very worrying,' Chiron said, rubbing his chin.

'Chiron, the arrival of the cyclops affected the weather,' Pappou added earnestly. 'Can you offer any suggestions?'

The centaur went quiet for a moment and tipped his head to one side, deep in thought. 'I would theorise it was connected to the transference of energy from one plane of existence to another.'

'That's what Oracle thought,' Pappou said.

'Plane of existence?' Theo asked, suddenly lost.

'I've not really explained the Net to him yet,' Pappou said, looking at Chiron.

'You've used the Sword of Chronos,' Chiron said, 'so you know that time is not a constant. That we can travel backwards through it, and even re-write it.'

'Yes,' Theo said.

'Although we call it the God Shield,' Chiron continued, 'this village is not protected by some invisible energy field that surrounds us.'

'Like I've seen in sci-fi films.'

'Exactly,' Chiron said.

'So, how is it protected?'

Chiron smiled, obviously pleased that he had Theo's attention. 'In this valley we are one second behind everyone else on Earth. This renders us invisible.'

'Because you are in ever so slightly in the past,' Theo said.

'Exactly, Kyrios ton Pithon. You catch on quickly.'

'And the Net is the same?' Theo asked, feeling happy that he'd worked it out.

'Not exactly. In the Net, time is caught in a constant loop. There is nothing but darkness. It is a terrible prison for the ones who are held there. They exist, but that is all. There is no joy, no music, no family, no community. There is nothing that would constitute a life,' Chiron said.

Theo was about to ask another question when there came a hammering on the front door.

'Come,' Chiron called towards the door.

It opened and a centaur appeared, her front hooves scraping the ground impatiently, or perhaps nervously. 'My Lord,' she said, 'movement has been spotted at the edges of the God Shield.'

CHAPTER TWELVE

Before anyone could ask the messenger any questions, a gong rang loud and insistent from outside.

'It's the alarm. We're in trouble,' Chiron snapped as he galloped over to the wall and took up the bow and quiver. 'Gongs are placed through the forest at equal intervals. It is the only side we are vulnerable to attack. Stay in here where you will remain safe. My warriors will already be taking up position. The enemy, whoever they are, will *not* get past the training field, let alone enter the village.'

Chiron slipped the quiver over his head and rushed out the open door without saying another word and disappeared with the messenger.

'I'm not staying here,' Theo said as soon as they were gone. He reached into his pocket, grabbed the hilt of the Sword of Chronos and extended the blade.

'Neither am I,' Pappou said.

'But you have nothing to protect yourself with,' said Theo, though he was more worried about how stiff his grandfather had become recently. 'You'd better stay here.'

The old man shook his head. 'Not happening. I'm still a Guardian. Besides, I have you to watch my back, and *I* can watch yours.'

'Or you can be something else for me to worry abou—'

Theo was cut off by screams from the village.

'There's no time to debate this,' Theo said, and ran over to the open doorway, looking into the darkness outside. He could just see over the tops of the houses in the village to the opposite, wooded side of the valley. A hundred or so metres away, the attackers were running out of the trees and down the training field, firing bows. The centaurs were already forming a defensive line, ready to stop the invaders from getting any further.

Theo recognised the hostile force straight away.

Arachne.

Like the centaurs, their bodies were made from two halves. Most of their body was a huge spider and, just like the centaurs, a human torso rose up from the front of it.

Theo dashed out the door, sword in hand and ran straight through the village, towards the communal fire. By the time he got to the middle ring of buildings, frightened centaurs were careening towards him, away from the fire, away from the attackers.

Theo, to your right—

Theo skidded to a halt, obeying Theseus's command, horrified by what he saw. A centaur was fighting an arachne in the middle of the road. The villager looked old and weak. Behind her, the front door to a house was open. A young centaur, about the size of a lamb, hid in the doorway, its eyes full of fear.

'Leave them alone!' Theo bellowed.

Before Theo could move, the arachne swiped the centaur's legs up from under her with a staff. The centaur crashed to the ground. As soon as she was down, the arachne used its eight hairy legs to pound her. It turned to look at Theo, a taunting smile across its lips.

Theo glared into the arachne's eyes, which glowed an evil shade of crimson, and charged. He brought the Sword of Chronos up ready to strike but the beast scuttled away from its victim.

Theo stopped beside the poor centaur. Her eyes looked up at him, filled with pain and fear. As Theo crouched beside her, she let out a rattling breath, and then stopped moving.

Theo's body filled with hate. A bellow burst from his mouth and the arachne moved further away, each of its long, hairy legs moving slowly and deliberately, the smile still on its lips. Summoning the heroes' power, Theo dashed forward, leaping into the air towards it, the sword raised above his head.

Then the arachne did something he was not expecting.

It turned and ran.

Theo landed on the street, the blade of the Sword of Chronos slicing into the cobbles. Theo pulled the blade free and prepared to fight, but the arachne had disappeared.

Why has it run? Theo wondered.

'Is my granny...?' came a trembling voice from behind Theo.

He turned and retracted the blade on the Sword of Chronos. The foal was standing behind him, stroking his grandmother's body. A tear slipped from the corner of Theo's eye as he knelt beside the foal. He felt the young creature lean against him, his body shaking as he began to cry.

A wave of panicked villagers came hurtling around the corner, away from the bonfire in the centre of the village. They scattered in every direction, heading for their homes.

The young centaur separated himself from Theo and ran over to an approaching adult, who knelt down and threw his arms around him. Theo stood numbly and watched as the two embraced.

'Come, we should leave them to grieve, and there's more to be done or there'll be other families suffering like them,' said Pappou, as he came around the corner, finally catching up with him.

'Why is this happening?' Theo asked as more panicked centaurs rushed down the street.

'I don't know,' Pappou answered as he pulled up alongside him. 'This has never happened before. Not only has the location of this place been exposed, but these terrible things have somehow escaped the Net.'

'Pappou, stay here and help this family. I've got to go.'

Before his grandfather could argue, Theo ran towards the centre of the village, past panicked parents, frightened children and the elderly. Theo ran past the fire and toppled furniture. He ran past it all. None of it mattered. What did matter was getting to the other side of the village and stopping the arachne from getting any further.

Theo's legs slowed beneath him as a thought occurred to him. If the arachne had come from the forest, how had the one he'd already seen got past the centaur warriors and so deep into the village?

Up! Look up! Theseus cried inside Theo's mind.

Theo did as he was instructed just as an arachne leapt down from the roof of a house, blocking his path. Unlike the other one, this arachne was armed with swords. It stabbed at Theo. With a simple thought, Theo activated his sword and their weapons rang out as they clashed together. The blow was so powerful, the vibrations ran down the blade and straight into Theo's hand. He gritted his teeth and clung on to the hilt.

'Die, human,' hissed the arachne, its long hairy legs thrusting out with each syllable.

Theo relaxed his grip on the sword and got ready

for the next attack. The arachne moved closer, its body swaying from side-to-side with each of its eight-legged steps.

'Scared, little boy?' it hissed, leaning his human half forward at the waist and jabbing his blades at Theo.

'No,' Theo answered.

'You look it. Don't worry. It's not *you* we want.'

Theo lunged forward with the Sword of Chronos. The arachne crossed its pair of swords to make an 'X' and blocking him.

Screams came from inside the house his attacker had leapt down from. Theo tried to look through the window but he couldn't get a clear line-of-sight past his opponent.

A loud trumpeting sound filled the air and Theo's opponent unexpectedly backed away. It climbed up the wall, its body covering the window.

'Our work here is done. Thanks for your help, young fool,' the arachne hissed, and then scampered up, uncovering the window.

Theo ran to it and looked inside. Everything was in disarray. And whoever had been screaming was no longer there. Leaping through the window, Theo narrowly missing an upturned table. Just like Chiron's, the house was one large room. And it was empty of centaurs and arachne.

Sprinting across the room, Theo left the house and ran back out onto the street.

'Theo, look!'

It was Pappou. He had caught up with him again. He pointed towards Chiron's house — back the way they had come. Back towards the cliff that rose up behind it. Ten or so arachne were climbing up the rock wall. They were different from the others. Each had a white spot on their backs.

'I've a bad feeling about this,' Theo said.

Turning around, Theo looked back toward the battle that was raging on the training field. A large group of arachne must have distracted and held back Chiron and his army, while a smaller strike force had sneaked in and taken... What?

Theo ran. Back into the side of the village he had started on. But it was no good, the fleeing arachne were just too fast and he was too far away from the cliff. If only they had stayed at Chiron's house as they had been ordered, perhaps he and Pappou could have stopped them.

'Pappou, get Chiron. Get anyone you can find!" Theo cried over his shoulder as he continued running, even though the arachne were getting higher and higher up the cliff. Heart racing and covered in sweat, Theo pumped his arms, driving his legs on, refusing to give up.

A bright flash of red light reflected off the cliff face. Then another and another. Theo's heart raced faster, but not because he was pushing himself. He'd seen the flashes before. They were the same as the ones that accompanied the minotaur last summer.

The arachne were gone, far away through time and space.

But what had they taken?

CHAPTER THIRTEEN

Behind Theo, the sounds of war from the training field stopped. The arachne who were attacking there must have also teleported out, their role complete. Then, loud and triumphant, came the cheer from the centaur warriors.

There was a moment of silence and then a new noise began. Only this time, it was much more terrible.

From all around him, Theo heard stunned, tortured cries coming from inside the centaur homes. Several centaurs came dashing out with spider silk wrapped around at least one of their limbs. Some had silk over their mouths stopping them from calling out.

'What's happened?' Theo asked.

'Our children! They've taken our children!' answered a staggering centaur, clearly in shock.

Theo looked up at the empty cliff face. The white bundles? They children must have been in them. Theo watched as more and more wailing centaurs came outside.

Suddenly it became too much and Theo leaned against a wall. This fight had been different from anything he had faced before. This wasn't some exciting adventure through time and space where he battled an opponent one-on-one, a challenge that was usually about tricking them through a portal.

This was war. People had been killed and injured. Children had been kidnapped.

'They just appeared and took my baby sister. There was nothing I could do,' came a stunned voice from behind Theo. He turned and looked at a young, female centaur. She looked about his age. Certainly too large to be carried away. 'Are you the Kyrios ton Pithon? Are you the one everyone was talking about around the fire before the attack began? You will help us, won't you?'

'I—' Theo began, but then he found himself unable to make the promise she wanted to hear. Instead, he lowered his sword and said, 'It wasn't your fault.'

'How did they find us?' she continued. 'How did they get through the God Shield?' Her face was pale, her words full of shock.

'Chiron's here!' a male voice called out as their leader charged through the village towards them, a host of warriors behind him.

'Our children! They've taken our children!' cried stricken parents, as they surged towards him.

'What shall we do? Chiron, tell us,' said another distraught centaur.

'Everyone, move away from the human,' Chiron shouted, as he slowed down from a gallop and came to a halt. The guards quickly formed a circle around Theo and the female centaur he had been talking to.

'Chiron, what are you doing?' Theo asked, his head darting around as he searched for Pappou.

'Let's start by answering this young lady's question,' the centaur leader replied. He took the young centaur's hand and guided her to the other side of the circle, *away* from Theo. 'How *did* they find us here, Kyrios ton Pithon?'

Theo didn't like the tone in the centaur leader's voice.

'I have no idea, but I promise we will get Oracle onto it immediately,' Theo answered, trying to see past Chiron and his warriors so he could search for Pappou.

'You have every idea, traitor,' Chiron said, glancing at the gathered crowd, 'because you're working with them.'

'What?' Theo stammered, shocked that the wise centaur would even make such a claim. 'I've been helping you.'

'Helping? You were told to wait at my house. No doubt you told the enemy you were the only ones there and it would be the best place to launch their ambush from. Your helping is just a careful ruse to cover your deceit. We've been hidden here for almost three thousand years. No one has ever found us. Ever.' Chiron stopped talking for a moment and stepped closer. With barely disguised anger, he stared down at Theo using his greater height and added, 'Until *you* came.'

'How can that be true?' Theo said. 'I've never even been here before, how could I lead them to you?'

'With a cleverly laid trap.' Chiron held out his hand. Theo's mobile phone lay in his palm. A blue light flashed in the corner. 'This is what led them here. This gift that you gave in the name of friendship. You are a traitor, and this is a traitor's Trojan horse.'

'Traitor!' the crowd screamed from behind the wall of warriors.

Theo almost laughed, with relief. If this was Chiron's reason, he could quickly correct him. 'It's just a message,' Theo said, pointing at the light. 'Why would I want to hurt you? I'm the Kyrios ton Pithon. It's my duty to protect you.'

Chiron ignored Theo and swiped his fingers across the screen. 'Let's see what it says. "I'm bored. Do you want to meet up?"' Chiron read aloud. A look of disappointment flashed across his face. 'Mia? Who is this Mia?'

'A friend of mine.'

A male voice from outside the circle shouted, 'It's a trick, oh great leader. Don't listen to him. Someone must pay. Our children…our children are gone.'

'It must be him. Who else could it be?' another centaur shouted.

More cries of outrage came. Theo noticed the warriors were being jostled by angry parents on the outside of the circle they had formed. The centaurs were turning into a mob and they were looking for someone to blame.

'I didn't do anything wrong,' Theo called, hoping everyone would hear him over the noise. 'Chiron, listen to reason. If I was helping the enemy, why would I send Pappou to get you?'

'It was already too late to save the children. It was a simple misdirection.'

The cries and wails from outside the circle grew louder.

'He did it.'

'He must pay!'

'Let me through!' cried a new voice. Theo felt himself relax a little at the sound of his grandfather's voice. He would be able to convince Chiron, surely? They'd known each other for what, fifty years?

Pappou forced his way through the defensive wall. The centaur warriors were clearly not sure whether to stop him or not. 'Chiron? What's going on?' Pappou demanded.

'We are discussing the possibility that your grandson is a traitor.'

'What? Don't be ridiculous,' Pappou said, in outrage as he made his way across the circle to stand by Theo's side.

'Don't listen to him,' came a voice from outside, a whole host of others voicing their agreement.

'He could be a spy too. He's been coming here for years.'

'Secretly gathering information about us.'

'Our numbers.'

'Our tactics.'

'He's not one of us.'

More echoes of agreement went up. Chiron raised his hand and the gathered mob went quiet.

'Chiron,' Theo said. 'Your people are afraid. I understand that, but I've done nothing wrong.'

'And neither have I,' added Pappou.

'Don't listen to them. We need to be sure,' another centaur cried, followed by cheers and further calls of agreement.

'I'm sorry, Xever,' Chiron said, his head bowed.

'Sorry for what?' Pappou asked.

'Take them prisoner and lock them up,' Chiron called to the warriors who were gathered around him. 'We need to investigate this further. Ourselves. Not Oracle. Not your servants, Kyrios ton Pithon.'

'Now wait a minute!' cried Pappou. 'Listen to yourself, Chiron. You are renowned for your skill, patience and wisdom. Where is the wisdom in what you're saying? Where is your patience? You must see this is just a coincidence. Don't let yourself be swayed by the crowd.'

'There are no such things as coincidences,' the centaur leader rumbled.

'Lord Chiron,' said a centaur. The warriors parted and another entered the circle.

'What is it, Klopian?'

'There's no trace of the enemy, but we found this.' Klopian held something out. It was a golden coin, ancient-looking and rough around the edges. A fragment of web clung to its edge.

'One of them must have dropped it!' Theo said desperately. 'It's a clue. Give me the coin and I will use it to track down the arachne.'

'That isn't going to happen. *You* are under arrest, remember?'

'I'm the Kyrios ton Pithon,' Theo said, stepping closer to Chiron. Around them, several warriors thrust their lances forward. Theo ignored them and carried on. 'It's my job to protect the Earth from escaped beasts. As you are on Earth that means you're included in that protection. And they,' Theo turned and pointed at the cliff, 'were escaped beasts. I *will* investigate this, and I *will* find your young ones and bring them back.' Theo paused long enough to soften his voice and added, 'I promise.'

'Chiron, are you really going to imprison Zeus' chosen champion? Don't you think he would have something to say about that?' Pappou said.

Chiron went quiet and surveyed the faces of the crowd of centaurs around him. His face changed. Was he finally listening to reason? If Chiron was intent on putting them in prison, Theo would grab Pappou, open a portal and escape. But that wouldn't help to convince Chiron that he was innocent.

'You can't let them go, great Chiron,' someone called. 'Not until we have answers.'

Cries of agreement followed.

Chiron let out a sigh and said, 'Give him the coin, Klopian. Here, take this infernal thing too.' Chiron handed over Theo's phone.

'No! You can't let them go,' cried the angry, frightened parents.

'Thank you, Lord Chiron,' Pappou said. 'We will get to the bottom of this.'

'Don't thank me yet, Xever. I give you two days to prove that the Kyrios ton Pithon had nothing to do with this.'

'I didn't,' Theo insisted.

'However, I cannot simply let you go without some form of insurance.' Chiron stepped back, threw back his head and shouted, 'I call upon the gods. Hear my words.'

'Yes, do it!' the crowd cried.

'Chiron, what are you doing?' Pappou said, stepping closer to his friend, his voice full of fear.

'Oh Hades, I pledge my life in exchange for a curse.'

'Chiron? No!' Pappou snapped.

'If this boy, Kyrios ton Pithon, is lying, or failed in his duty as guardian, I surrender my life in order to curse his.'

'What's going on?' Theo asked. 'Pappou?'

Pappou didn't answer, he just took Theo's arm and

pulled him away. 'Why, Chiron? Why did you do that, you fool?'

'Do what?' Theo asked, confused.

'I have placed a curse on you and your family. A curse will ensure you will do as you have promised. If you *are* innocent,' Chiron said it like it was a dirty word, 'I shall release you.'

'A curse?' Theo said.

'Bad luck, or even death itself, will follow you around,' explained Chiron. 'And, if in two days you cannot bring me proof of your innocence, it will strike on you, boy, and all who carry the Bloodline of Theseus.'

CHAPTER FOURTEEN

Theo was glad to be back in the Hall of Heroes and away from the anger of the centaurs. He couldn't believe the sense of relief he felt when Chiron let him and Pappou go.

The soft green glow from the torches mounted on the wall of the cave helped to make him feel at ease. There was something special about the place. Theo remembered the comforting feeling he'd felt the first time he'd come here, even though he was in the dark, in a place he didn't recognise, and he'd just fled the minotaur.

'Right,' Pappou said, leaning against the table and letting out a deep breath. 'Where do you suggest we start?'

Theo felt relieved that Pappou wanted to get on with things. He was terrified of the curse, but he didn't want to talk about. Not at the moment, anyway.

'I think it's got to be the coin,' Theo suggested, removing it from his pocket.

'Have you seen one before on your journeys with your mother?' Pappou asked.

Theo shook his head.

'I'm sorry to interrupt,' said Oracle, 'but if you would care to keep me informed, I may be able to help you.'

'Sorry, Oracle. We've just come from quite a tense situation,' said Pappou.

'So I see.'

'What do you mean?' asked Theo.

'It would appear Chiron is in communication with Our High Lord Zeus.'

Theo closed his eyes. The situation was getting worse. He'd already annoyed Zeus once.

'Try not to worry,' Pappou said, holding out his hand. 'We've got a job to do. Now, let's look at that coin.'

Theo handed it over and Pappou placed it on the cloth in the middle of the table. 'Oracle, can you scan it and create a 3D holographic image, so we can see it more easily?'

'Of course. Nothing could be simpler,' she answered.

A moment later, a larger version of the coin appeared, constructed of blue light and rotating above the table.

'Now, let's have a good look. Oracle, freeze the image,' ordered Pappou.

The plate-sized coin stopped spinning. Theo moved closer to the table and studied the hologram. The side he could see showed the image of a woman sitting at a loom and weaving cloth.

'That must be Arachne,' Theo said. 'She challenged Athena to a weaving contest and the goddess turned her into a half-spider-half-human as a punishment for being so big-headed and daring to challenge a god.'

Pappou smiled and placed his hand on his shoulder in that comforting way of his. 'See, all those stories I've told you are useful. Who won?'

'There are different versions. Sometimes Arachne, sometime Athena.'

Pappou's laughter filled the Hall of Heroes. Theo enjoyed the sound after so much tragedy and sadness. If there was anyone he could rely on to make things seem brighter, it was Pappou.

'Oracle, let's see the other side,' Theo said.

'Of course,' she answered. The coin flipped over, exposing the other side. It showed Arachne in her new form. She looked happy and proud of her eight legs.

'It doesn't look like Athena's punishment taught her anything,' said Theo. 'Oracle, can you tell us anything about the gold the coin is made from?'

'Good idea,' Pappou said.

'Yes, but this may be more interesting: the coin has a layer of temporal energy surrounding it,' she said.

'So, the arachne travelled through time as well as space to get inside the God Shield?' Theo asked.

'A reasonable assumption,' agreed Pappou.

'Can the levels of energy give us any idea where they came from?' Theo asked.

'Another great idea, Theo. Are you thinking the energy will be stronger the further they've travelled?'

Theo shrugged his shoulders, a little embarrassed by his grandfather's attention. Did he mean it, or was he just trying to make Theo feel better or take his mind off the curse? Theo decided it didn't really matter. Whatever he was doing, Pappou was only showing him how much he loved him.

'I shall begin calculating,' Oracle said, 'but the odds are that there will be many possible locations that could offer a viable starting point.'

'Maybe,' said Theo, 'but some will be more likely than others. For example, if the Net is one, then that's a good place to start.'

'That is one location I can confidently rule out,' Oracle said.

Theo waited for an explanation from her, but none came, so he asked why.

'The Net has a very particular energy signature, which I would pick up immediately.'

'So, these arachne are living where? Here on Earth?'

'That would seem to be the only available explanation.'

'But where?' Theo said, rubbing his chin.

'They could be hiding somewhere out of sight,' Pappou suggested.

'But there can't be many places left on Earth that

we can't see because of satellites and stuff,' said Theo, looking across at his grandfather, who was also rubbing his chin in thought.

'You'd think so, but that isn't true, as you've just found out. Besides, they could simply be in the past before satellites,' Pappou said.

'Of course,' Theo felt a little stupid for not thinking of something so obvious.

Pappou rubbed his hands together and said, 'Oracle, could they be using something like the God Shield?'

'Unlikely. Like the Net, it would leave a particular signature.'

'So, we've got nothing,' Theo said, stepping away from the table, the threat of the curse filling his every thought again.

'Oracle didn't say that,' Pappou said, encouragingly. 'Oracle, keep scanning the coin and see if you can lock down any possible locations.'

'Of course, Ninety-Eight.'

'Get in touch as soon as you discover something. I think it's time for us to go home.'

Theo sat in the kitchen at Pappou's house while his grandfather made a traditional Cypriot salad. Unlike most kids, Theo loved olives. Pappou was having a nice cup of tea, a habit he had picked up from his

English wife, years ago. Theo sipped at a glass of water.

'I'd better be going back home to Mum,' Theo said, finishing his drink.

'I'd tell you to send my love, but it would be difficult to explain.'

'Pappou, Mum thinks we talk over Skype every week,' Theo said, getting up and giving Pappou a hug. He wasn't sure, but Theo thought he heard the old man make a sharp intake of breath.

'Are you all right, Pappou?'

'I'm fine. I'm just getting old.'

Theo smiled and nodded, but now he had another thing to worry about. Pappou had just admitted what Theo had been fearing. Ever since his father had died, Pappou had been the male figure in his life and he'd always been a good role model. Especially over the last year.

'I better get going,' Theo said. He mumbled the incantation under his breath, created a portal and without looking at his grandfather again, stepped through it.

Theo wasn't ignoring his grandfather as he left, he just didn't want him to see him crying. Or where he had opened the portal to.

He stepped out into the bright sunshine. A strong wind tugged at his clothes. He was near the top of the

Troodos Mountains, standing a few metres away from the long winding road that went to the top and ended in a barricade. The ground beneath his feet, like most of Cyprus, was baked — the grass yellow, the soil grey and sand-like. Huge rocks and boulders rose out of the ground, aside from a few trees and shrubs, they looked like the only things that grew here.

If Theo had looked to his right he would have been able to see all the way down to Paphos, where Pappou lived, thirty or forty miles away. But he didn't look to the side. He stared straight ahead at the bend in the road.

Maybe it was the trees, maybe it had been the bright sunshine, or maybe his dad just hadn't been paying attention, but that very spot was where his father had had his fatal motorcycle accident.

Theo stared down at the sword in his hand. He could go back. He could save his dad. He had the power. It wasn't the first time he'd thought about it. And it wouldn't be the last. But he was forbidden from using the sword to change his own history. The way things were going, maybe it didn't matter if he angered Zeus or caused another time paradox. Because of the curse, he could be dead in less than two days.

Why had Chiron done something so reckless? With the help of Pappou and Oracle, Theo was sure they would solve the mystery or find some way out of the curse. Surely Zeus wouldn't let his chosen warrior die?

'Hello, Theo.'

Theo jumped at the sound of the voice. For a brief moment, images of his father filled his mind. Maybe it was ghost or something. Maybe it had all been a terrible mistake and his father had been alive and well and living like a hermit up in the mountains all this time.

It wasn't the first time Theo had had these thoughts, but he knew deep down the voice was too high to be a man's. What's more, he recognised it, even if it was a voice he had not heard for a year.

'Hello, Calista,' he said, without even looking at her.

CHAPTER FIFTEEN

'What brings you all the way up here?' Theo asked, turning around and eyeing the girl suspiciously.

'I was about to ask you the same thing,' Calista said with a smile, her dark eyes twinkling and dark hair floating about in the breeze. Like most natives of Cyprus, she was covered up to protect herself from the sun by a pair of jeans and a cream top that covered her arms. Only tourists and holiday-makers walked around in shorts and a t-shirt. It was how she had singled him out last summer despite his Cypriot-looking features.

'By the gods it's good to see you again. I was thinking you were ignoring me,' she said, stepping closer.

Theo deactivated the blade on the Sword of Chronos and put the hilt away. It was funny, now that he thought back to last summer, she had never reacted when he turned up and rescued her with all his god-powered artefacts. To her it all seemed normal, but then, perhaps it was. There was something strange, something mysterious, about Calista, but he'd never worked out what it was.

'How did you find me?' he asked. Strange and mysterious weren't the only words to describe Calista. Mischievous and secretive were two others, and Theo was not sure if he completely trusted her.

'Oh, I was just out for a walk and stumbled across you. The Troodos Mountains are magnificent, aren't they? But, if you're looking for the gods on Mount Olympus, this is the wrong one. Never mind, the view from up here is breathtaking.'

'I know this isn't *the* Mount Olympus.'

'Of course you do, Theo. Of course you do.'

'Why are you really here?'

'I just told you.'

And there it was. That was why he was never sure if he should trust her. She never really answered a question, and when she did…

'Why are you always so worried?' she asked.

'Because you always turn up—'

'When you need help?' Calista finished for him.

'Yes. No! That wasn't what I was going to say. I was going to say that you turn up and trouble follows.'

Calista laughed and tucked some of her wild hair behind her ear.

'And, by the way,' Theo continued, 'it was you that

disappeared, not me. So, if anyone's been ignoring anyone, it's you. I tried to find you before I went back to England last summer, but you were nowhere to be found. As usual.' Calista had this annoying habit of just...disappearing.

'True,' she said, shrugging her shoulders. 'Still, my mysterious side is part of my appeal, isn't it?'

Theo raised his eyebrows and said, 'Are you ever going to tell me anything about you?'

'That depends on what you want to know.'

'What's your connection to Ariadne? Let's start with that.'

When Theo first met Calista last summer they had played at The Tombs of the Kings a few times before having an adventure together. Part of his adventure was to travel back in time, defeat the minotaur and restore time. While in the past, Theo had met Ariadne at King Minos' palace. She had looked just like Calista, only a few years older. And now, a year later, Calista was starting to look as beautiful as Ariadne had.

'My connection to Ariadne? It's my Greek blood, I suppose. Dark hair, dark eyes. We must look quite similar.'

'No. You're much more than just similar. You have the same forehead and nose. The same cheeky smile.'

'Are you saying I have a big head?' she said, touching her forehead, but trying to make it look like she was tiding more wayward hair.

'That would be telling,' Theo replied, giving her a taste of her own medicine.

Calista sat down on a nearby rock and ignored his comment. 'Are you here visiting you father? You know, where he—'

Theo glared at her. 'How do you know about that?'

'You told me.'

'Did I?' Theo asked, narrowing his eyes. He couldn't remember. He didn't tend to talk about it. At school, after it happened, one of the teaching assistants had been sent on a special bereavement counselling course so she could help him work his way through it. She was a nice lady, but the pictures and stories they made to put in a memory jar seemed pointless. Dad was gone, and nothing was going to change that. Nothing.

Theo touched the sword hilt in his pocket. Some things could change that, even if they did come at a cost.

'Yes, this is where my dad died,' Theo said, staring at the tarmac road. 'Four years ago.'

'I remember.'

Theo turned and glared at her. 'How can you possibly remember? You didn't even know me then. Are you playing with me? Are you *trying* to upset me?'

'No,' Calista said, shaking her head. 'I'm sorry, I really am. Sometimes I find it difficult to connect with people.'

'A convenient excuse for being rude,' Theo snapped, suddenly realising he sounded just like his mother.

Now it was Calista's turn to go quiet. 'The thing is, I've seen too many things and I know too many things. It makes it hard sometimes, to be considerate, I mean.'

'Why can't you just be honest with me? Maybe that would help?' Theo said in a gentle tone.

'It might, but where's the fun in that?' Calista said, her dark mood already forgotten.

'So, I take it you're not going to tell me?'

'Tell you what?'

Theo sighed and went and sat beside her. The rock was warm from being in the sun all day. He took a deep, calming breath. He wanted answers, and the only way he would get them was to humour Calista, even if he got hurt in the process.

'How do you know this is where my dad died?'

'I...I felt it happen.'

'You felt it?' Theo said, confused.

'Yes. You wanted some honesty. I'll give you some. I am connected to your family. The Cypriot side, obviously.'

'Connected, how?' Theo wanted to ask if she was connected to the Guardians, but he didn't know how much she knew. He also remembered how Pappou had reacted when he had caught them chatting moments before she had been kidnapped by the minotaur. It felt like a long time ago now, but it seemed like Pappou didn't trust her either.

'Think about the bloodline of Theseus, but not *the* bloodline of Theseus.'

'You know about that?'

'Of course, I do. Come on, think about it, Theo, it's obvious, really.'

Theo went quiet. If she wasn't related to him, to Theseus then…

'You're from the bloodline of Ariadne.' Theo cried, leaping to his feet. 'Are you like me?'

'By the gods, I hope not,' she laughed. 'That's all I'm going to tell you. For now.'

'Are you on my side?' Theo asked, crossing his arms. 'Can I trust you?'

'Hmmmm. Let me think. Theseus dumped Ariadne on an island.'

'So Dionysus could marry her instead,' Theo protested.

'Only in some versions of the story. They were changed to make Theseus look less like a shallow, selfish pig.'

'He was a bit of a…' Theo paused and sat back down as he tried to find the right word to describe him. Luckily, the last three thousand years had changed Theseus a lot and he was now a valuable ally.

'Don't worry about all that,' Calista said. 'Let's just agree that just because they didn't work out it doesn't mean that we can't be friends.'

'Well, if we're friends, I need your help.'

'What is it this time?'

Theo quickly filled her in on what had happened in the centaur village except for the curse. It wasn't that he didn't trust her — sort of — but that she would probably turn it into some kind of joke.

'Are you talking about the camp hidden in Thessaly?' she asked.

'You know about it?'

'Why do you keep being surprised by what I know?'

'Why do you keep asking questions?'

'Why do you?'

Theo stared at her and didn't continue her silly game.

'Those poor children,' Calista said. 'Do you have any clues to go on?'

'Only this coin,' Theo said, handing it over.

'Arachne the weaver,' Calista said, her eyes narrowing.

'You look like you know something,' Theo said.

'I might be able to help you. Give me some time to see if I can check a few things out. Can I keep this?'

'It'll be a good test of loyalty, I suppose,' Theo said. He looked down at Aphrodite's Rock. Oracle had a complete scan of the coin back in the Hall. If Calista disappeared with it, hopefully it wouldn't be too much of a problem.

'You saved my life, remember. I owe you,' said Callista.

'Yes, I suppose you do,' Theo said, turning back to look at her.

He smiled.

As usual, she was gone.

CHAPTER SIXTEEN

Theo went back to England, making sure he returned to his bedroom a second after he had left it. He climbed into bed, and heard his grandparents leave just before he fell asleep.

The next morning Mum was gone by the time he awoke, but he could hear his grandparents talking downstairs. They also had the radio on. It was blaring away even though granddad insisted he wasn't deaf. Theo shouldn't complain. He and Mum wouldn't have coped without his Dad's parents.

He was about to get out of bed and go downstairs when he remembered the curse. He shut his eyes and willed the memory away. It didn't work, so he thought about Calista instead. Should he have trusted her with the coin? Then he thought about Pappou.

How did he end up with so many worries? This time last year, all he was worried about was starting year seven.

He got up, had a shower and got dressed.

'Morning, Theo. Breakfast?' Gran asked, as soon as he appeared in the kitchen.

'Morning. It's okay, I can sort myself out,' Theo said, sitting at the breakfast bar and pouring some cornflakes in a bowl. After he emptied it, he had another. He was hungrier than he thought, but then many hours had passed while he was in Cyprus and Greece, and he'd been busy. As he was discovering, life as a Guardian was not easy or simple.

'Have you got any plans today?' Gran asked, taking his empty bowl away.

'No, I—' he began, then he remembered Mia's text message. The one that had landed him in so much trouble. 'I might invite a friend around, if that's okay?'

'It's your house, love. Have we met him before?'

'It's a girl,' Theo said, feeling his cheeks go a little pink.

'Oh,' Gran said in a way that made him go even redder.

'We're just friends. We got on well at the holiday camp last week.'

'It'll be that girl with the weird hair, Pam,' Granddad said.

'Maybe I'll see if I can go to her house,' said Theo.

'Don't be like that. We're was only teasing. Sorry,' said Gran.

'You could go home if I went there. I'm sure you have things to do,' Theo suggested.

Gran screwed up her face. 'Oh, I'm not sure your mum would like that. Maybe you could arrange something for another day.'

Theo nodded and took his phone out of his pocket. He opened the message that Chiron had read out. He replied.

You can come over today, or if you prefer, I could come to you tomorrow.

Theo had barely put the phone down on the breakfast bar when it let out a *ding* and the little blue light flashed.

I really need to see you. Something weirds going on. I'll come to you. See you in 30.

'Gran, Mia's coming in thirty minutes, okay? I think we'll hang out in the tree house.'

'That's fine. Granddad and I were planning on doing the garden today anyway.'

'Great,' Theo said, though depending on what Mia had to say, he didn't really want them listening.

Theo looked around the tree house, dusted his hands on his jeans and smiled. It had needed a bit of a tidy up, but it was looking good now. He suspected Mia wouldn't be afraid of spiders, but there had been a lot of cobwebs. Gran had wanted to help him, but she found the ladder too tricky. Now she was in the garden with Granddad.

He loved his tree house, even if his head almost touched the ceiling now. The very first time he'd used the sword to create a portal, this was where he'd travelled to. It had special memories and emotions attached to it and Pappou had told him they were the easiest places to travel to when you started out.

And this place *was* special. Theo had designed and built it with his dad. They had finished it just before they went on holiday to Cyprus. The same holiday Dad had died. Dad never had the chance to enjoy it with him. Theo tried to not let that spoil the special place they had built together.

He watched the footpath down the side of the garden through the treehouse window, waiting for Mia to arrive. She appeared around the corner on the end of the street, dressed in black, her hair tied up to show off her undercut, a bright pink PVC backpack slung over her shoulder.

Throwing open the trapdoor in the middle of the treehouse floor, Theo climbed through the gap and made his way down the rope ladder. By the time he got to the ground, Mia was walking across the grass towards him.

'This is an amazing house,' Mia said, staring at the building and the garden. 'You must be rich!'

'Morning,' Theo said by way of greeting and

added, 'Mum has a good job and Dad's life insurance paid off the mortgage so...' Theo didn't finish the sentence. If he had the choice, he would rather live in a tiny flat and still have his dad.

'Life insurance?'

'Yes, my dad died."

'Sorry,' Mia said. 'Me and my big mouth.'

'It's okay. You didn't know.'

'Hello,' Gran said as she walked over from the flower border she had been weeding. 'I'm Theo's gran, but you can call me Pam. And that miserable old thing is Roger, Theo's granddad.'

'I heard that!' Granddad said.

'Thought you were deaf,' Gran called back. 'Theo's a terrible host. Can I get you a drink, Mia?'

'Thanks. Can I have some water, please.'

'We have pop and squash.'

'No, thanks. I'm fussy about what I put in my body. I'm a vegetarian.'

'Oh, right,' Gran said, slowly. 'I'll get you some water. Theo?'

'I'll have the same. Remember to use those cups with the lids.'

'Yes, sir,' Gran said and walked through the patio door and into the house.

'This way,' Theo said, and walked back over to oak tree in the middle of their huge lawn. 'I hope you don't mind heights.'

'You have a tree house?' Mia said, her eyes sparkling. 'No way.'

By the time they had climbed in, Gran had reappeared at the bottom of the tree with their drinks.

'This is so cool,' Mia said, looking around at the posters Theo had put up.

'Thanks,' Theo said, picking up a basket that was tied to a length of rope. He lowered it down. Mia leant forward and watched Gran put the two cups into the basket. She gave a thumbs up and Theo pulled the rope up until the basket was inside. He sealed the trap door.

'It's cozy up here,' Mia said, sitting cross-legged on the floor.

'When me and Dad built it, we forgot that I'd grow. There used to be a little table and chairs, but now I have to sit on the floor.'

'It's cool, I always sit like this.'

Theo nodded, and they fell into silence.

Great, Theo thought. *We've already run out of things to say.*

'Theo,' Mia said, eventually. 'She looked like she wanted to say something important — something awkward or embarrassing.

'What is it?' he asked, not looking forward to her answer.

'Ever since we went away, I've been having...'

'What?' Theo said.

'I've been having these dreams. You're in them and...'

'And?' Theo asked. Then it occurred to him. Did she fancy him? Theo liked her, but not like that. Besides, he was too busy to get involved with girls.

'And,' she said, pausing to take a breath, 'you had a sword and you fought a giant, one-eyed monster.'

Theo couldn't help the sharp intake of breath he made. 'What? What did you say?'

'I've been having dreams where you've been fighting a one-eyed giant. Look.' Mia reached into her pocket. She took out a piece of paper, unfolded it and smoothed it out on the floor next to her.

Theo looked at it for a moment and then moved a little closer. 'You're a great artist,' was all he could think to say as he picked up the picture, stunned.

'Thanks. I've drawn this picture so many times, I feel like I'm becoming a master.'

The picture was incredible. She had Akanthus down in every perfect little detail — his crooked teeth, the creases and wrinkles about his eye, the ragged sheepskin clothing.

'How many times have you drawn this?'

'Seven. The first time was in the middle of the night. I woke up to find my parents hovering above me. I'd been calling out in my sleep, apparently. They said I was talking nonsense, but I was very loud and kept saying it over and over. They thought it would stop, but when it didn't, they came in to wake me.'

'And then what happened?' Theo asked, half-curious, half-alarmed. This was amazing. And frightening. How had this happened? Had Lola and the others experienced the same dreams? Lola's encounter with

Akanthus was much worse than anyone else — except maybe the shepherd.

Mia continued. 'As soon as my parents left me alone, I went to my desk and started to draw what I'd seen in the dream. It all happened by the waterfall, you know where we had that photograph taken, but there was snow everywhere. And you...you had a sword.'

'Weird,' Theo said, unsure what else to say.

'Yes. What's strange,' Mia went on, 'is that I never remember my dreams, but this time, I remembered it all, and the more I thought about it, the more and more I remembered.'

Theo felt his face go pale. He reached out to grab his cup of water so he could hide his face behind it. Noticing his hand was shaking, he quickly put the cup down before Mia saw.

'Sounds pretty vivid,' he said.

'Are you okay?' Mia asked.

'Yeah,' he replied.

'I stayed up for an hour, drawing the picture three times. I was exhausted, so I climbed back into bed. I don't remember falling asleep, but I had the dream again.'

'Tell me exactly what happened.'

'Well, it was snowing, like I said, and we were walking down the steps towards the waterfall.'

'The others were in the dream too?'

'Yes, I was with Amanda, Lola, Faroq, Alfie and Hector. We'd already been to the top of the hill and met this creepy shepherd. On the way back he'd disappeared but his quad bike was still there, only it was tipped on its side.'

'By the waterfall,' Theo said, deliberately pretending to misunderstand. This was all getting too complicated. With two versions of events, he had to make sure he didn't get them muddled up.

'No, it was on the top of the hill,' she said pointing her finger at the picture. 'We were on a walk and it started to snow, so Daniel told us to go back.'

'Right,' Theo said, a sinking feeling in his stomach. This couldn't be a coincidence. Could it? What was it that Chiron had said about coincidences? Was this the beginning of the curse? Was this how his life was going to be ruined? Chiron did say it didn't have to be death.

'So, we were walking down the footpath back to the waterfall when we heard this terrible bellow and from out of the snow came...well...this,' she said tapping the picture again. 'We ran and hid, but the others, who were behind us, turned around and went back towards you and Daniel. You were at the back having a cosy chat.

Theo almost said 'It was anything but cosy' when he realised he would give himself away.

'The thing ran off up the steps, chasing after Ali, Oskar and the other girls. Somehow it didn't see us hiding behind a snow-covered bush.'

'That was lucky,' said Theo.

'Amanda told us to run, and we were about to

move when the thing came flying back down the stairs and crashed onto the ground. I'd swear I felt the whole place shake. The next minute you appeared, with this sword in your hand.' Mia stopped talking and swung her backpack off her shoulder. The zip was loud in the silence of the tree house. She handed Theo another picture.

Theo's eyes went wide in amazement. It was a picture of the Sword of Chronos, accurate to the smallest detail — the three heads of Chronos, the man, the bull and the lion — the snake handle, even the unusual shape of the blade.

'This is *some* wild dream, Mia,' Theo said, with a nervous laugh.

'That's the thing. When I went back to sleep, it happened all over again, and it was exactly the same. Except this time there was more. We all hid in the bushes and watched as you fought the thing. I don't even know what it's called.'

'A cyclops,' Theo said, putting the picture of the sword down and picking up the one of Akanthus.

'Yes, I remember now. We did it in year five. The Odyssey. Is that right?'

Theo nodded.

Mia carried on. 'You fought it. Or tried to. He had a huge club — an old tree stump he just ripped up out of the ground — and then you ran away down the path away from everyone else. The cyclops stood there looking in the direction you had gone and then at the stairs where Ali and the others had escaped.

That was when Amanda decided that we had to get away too, while he was distracted. We ran. I was terrified. We started down the stairs when we came round this huge bolder and—'

'That is too crazy,' Theo interrupted her. 'Come on, why don't we go and—'

'Theo, I've got more to tell you. I drew the cyclops again, and the sword, and this...' She reached into her bag again and handed over a folded-up piece of paper.

Theo held it in his shaking hand and stared down at it.

'Aren't you going to open it?' Mia said.

Theo looked at Mia as he folded back the paper.

His eyes went wide. It was a disaster.

It was him, throwing a punch, while around him was the ghostly outline of the cyclops the Medallion of Morpheus had created.

'W—what's this?' Theo said.

'After you ran away, you came back, only you were disguised as another cyclops. At first I didn't realise — your disguise was almost perfect — but the more I looked, I could see you inside it, controlling it like a puppeteer. You managed to convince the other one you were his cousin, Polyphemus, and that he should let us all go.'

Theo swallowed. He remembered her staring into his eyes. He'd thought it was a coincidence but…

'That really is a crazy dream,' Theo said, getting up off the floor and looking out the window as he decided what to say next. It looked like his grandparents were arguing about a plant or something. There was a lot of pointing and head-shaking going on.

'But that's the thing, Theo,' Mia said. 'I'm not sure it *was* a dream.'

CHAPTER SEVENTEEN

'What do you mean? Not a dream?' Theo said, turning away from the tree house window and looking at her.

'For a start I remember it. I remember it *all*. And that never happens. I might remember the end of a dream or the basic ideas, but I remembered all of this,' she said, tapping her pictures. 'This is like it really happened and somehow I forgot.'

'It was quite scary, for a dream,' Theo suggested, feeling his throat go dry. 'Maybe that's why you've remembered it so well.'

'But that's not all. If I concentrate, I can...I can see two versions of that afternoon. The one where it was sunny and bright, and there was no weird shepherd and certainly no cyclops. But then, I remember this too,' she said pointing at the picture. 'How can I have two different memories of the same day?'

'You can't, it's impossible,' Theo said, even though he did too. 'Have you spoken to the others about it?'

Mia shook her head.

'Don't. They'll think you're crazy,' he quickly added.

'Do you think I'm crazy, Theo?'

Theo had to sit down, if he didn't, he was going to fall down. What was happening? It wasn't a dream. He knew it. So how could she remember what happened the first time they went to the waterfall?

Then an answer came to him. Calista.

Back when he had seen the minotaur the first time in Tomb 6A, the past had been changed and so had the layout of the tomb. Calista had somehow been able to remember both the old and the new, the way the tomb looked before Pappou tricked the minotaur into knocking down some of the pillars as well as the way it looked now.

Calista was from the Bloodline of Ariadne.

Could there be something special about Mia too? Was that why she could remember it all? Was that why she could see through the illusion of the Medallion of Morpheus?

Suddenly, Theo had an idea. A way of testing her.

'Well, do you?' Mia said.

Theo looked at her like a rabbit caught in a path of an angry cyclops' club. She had obviously been talking to him while he was miles away in his thoughts. 'Do I what?'

'Do you think I'm crazy?'

Theo picked up the picture of him disguised as Polyphemus. 'Do you really think this happened?'

'I don't think it happened. I know it,' she said, tapping her head.

'Maybe you *do* know it or...you're going crazy,' Theo laughed nervously.

Mia flung her arm out, her chucky bracelet sliding up her arm because she moved so fast. The tips of her fingers whipped Theo's upper arm.

'Ow!' he cried, quickly rubbing it.

'Don't call me crazy,' she said, smiling.

'Now that's the Mia I know, I was beginning to think you had turned into someone else.'

'Very funny.'

'I need to get something,' Theo said. 'Wait here, okay?'

'Sure. But I might have a snoop around.'

'Feel free, but there's not a lot up here anymore.'

'Oh, I'm sure I'll find some kind of secret.'

Theo opened the trap door and climbed down the rope ladder. He walked across the immaculate lawn, past his grandparents and towards the patio doors as calmly as he could and disappeared into the house. Taking the steps two at a time, he raced up the stairs and into his bedroom. He shut the door, threw his back against it and let out the breath he had been holding the whole way there.

Once his heart-rate settled back to normal, he went to his desk and pulled out the drawer with the false bottom. He scooped it out and paused. He was going to talk to Pappou, but he already knew what his grandfather would say.

'Don't tell her a thing. Ignore it and hope it goes away. I'll speak to Zeus and get it fixed.'

'But what if she's like me and Calista?' Theo thought aloud. It would be good to have someone to share his secret life with, right? He couldn't tell Mum, and he couldn't keep going to Cyprus to talk to Pappou every time he had an idea or was worried about something. Sooner or later Mum would catch him using the sword, and even though he tried to return to his bedroom a second after he left it, all it needed was for Mum to walk in at the wrong moment. There was Calista to talk to, but she was...difficult.

Every hero had a friend they could count on. Perhaps for him it could be Mia. If only he knew her a little better.

Theo stepped away from the desk and sat down on his bed. It was time to try the idea he had in the tree house. He quickly grabbed his phone off the desk and sent a message to Mia.

Faroq's coming round. I've told him to join you in the tree house. I'll be up soon.

Theo waited for the *ping* to inform him that Mia had replied. He looked out of his bedroom window and straight at the tree house. Gran and Granddad were nowhere to be seen.

His phone still hadn't pinged, so he went back downstairs.

'I was going to make some sandwiches for lunch,' Gran called as he passed through the kitchen.

'Brilliant,' Theo answered and went into the dining room and out the patio doors. As he did, he summoned the power of the Medallion. If Mia could really see through its power she wouldn't fall for his next trick.

He climbed up the rope ladder and popped his head through the trap door. Mia had her back to him, she was looking between two overlapping pieces of wood, clearly trying to see if Theo had hidden anything there.

'Hi, Mia,' he said to her back. 'What are you doing?'

'Just being nosey, Faroq.'

Theo smiled. It had worked. As soon as he'd passed his grandparents he'd got the medallion to change his appearance.

Mia turned to face him, let out a little cry of surprise and jumped. 'Don't do that, Theo.'

'It's me, Faroq,' Theo said, his heart sinking.

'You might sound like Faroq, but you don't look like him. I can see it's you, Theo. And that floppy fringe does not suit you — at all.'

Theo climbed up through the trapdoor and deactivated the medallion.

'How do you do that?' Mia asked. 'That's amazing!

It was like you had a ghost of Faroq over the top of you.'

Theo looked at her, trying to make up his mind what to do. To Tartarus with it, he decided. He reached down the front of his t-shirt and pulled out the Medallion of Morpheus.

'What's that?' Mia said, going to reach for it. She stopped, her finger tips just a few centimetres from it, and pulled her hand back.

'It's what allows me to change what I look like. Watch.'

Theo closed his eyes and imagined he was Alfie, Lola, and then Daniel. He could tell it was working because of Mia's reaction. Her face said it all. She was amazed. And repulsed.

'Stop it, that's weird, especially when you're a girl. So, it wasn't a dream. I do remember two different versions of the day.'

Theo nodded. 'For some reason this doesn't work properly on you.'

'Hang on, I don't understand. Rewind a bit.'

'Look, sit down,' Theo said, sitting on the floor next to her. Suddenly all his nerves had disappeared. It felt good to tell someone all about his secret. He hadn't realised it had been such a weight on his shoulders. 'All I have to do is imagine I'm someone else and the medallion does something to your brain and tricks you. Or it's supposed to. Would you like to try?' Theo asked, leaning forward, ready to slide the medallion chain over her head.

'I don't think so, I'm quite happy with who I am,' she said, moving backwards. 'But, the sword I saw you with. Can I see that?'

'Erm...' Theo said. He had opened the floodgates now and from what he knew about Mia, there was no way she would give up until she got what she wanted.

'Go on. I won't tell anyone. This will be just between you and me. You trust me, don't you?'

'Well...'

'Cheers!' Mia said, getting to her feet. 'I trusted you. I came here and told you about how my brain is filled with two different days and—'

'Okay,' Theo said. 'But you must promise not to tell anyone.'

'Of course,' Mia said, smiling.

Theo wasn't sure, but it was too late to stop now. Wasn't it? 'Wait here and I'll be back soon.'

'Don't worry, I'm not going anywhere.'

Theo scrambled down the rope ladder and went through the patio doors.

'The sandwiches are ready,' Gran called out.

'Great! I'm just getting something and then we'll come and eat,' Theo shouted as he ran up the stairs and entered his room. He found the hilt of The Sword of Chronos under the mattress and wrapped his fingers around it, feeling it move and grow to fit his hand perfectly. Stashing the bronze handle in the small backpack he had taken to the Lake District, Theo headed back downstairs.

'What are you doing? You're up and down like a yo-yo,' Gran said.

'Very funny,' Theo said without pausing.

'What have you got in the bag?' Gran asked just as Theo was about to go through the patio doors.

'Nothing, why?'

'Nothing?'

'Yes,' Theo said, suddenly wishing he hadn't lied.

'Good,' Gran said. 'Come here.'

'Why?'

'You might as well put these sandwiches in it and take them up with you. I've put them in a plastic container for you. Here's a can of pop and a bottle of water for Mia, unless you want to bring her down here so we can say hello.'

Theo walked back into the kitchen, unzipped the top of the bag and loaded the food and drinks in. 'No, you're okay, Gran.'

'I understand,' Gran said with a wink and a smile.

'She's *just* a friend,' Theo said over his shoulder as he made his way to the patio doors.

'That's what your dad said about your mum.'

Theo stopped and shook his head at his grandmother.

A few moments later he was back in the tree house.

'Didn't you bring it?' Mia asked, looking disappointed.

Theo emptied the bag of the things Gran had made, and then brought out the sword, laying it in the flat of his palm.

'Is...is it moving?' Mia said, screwing up her face.

Theo laughed. 'Yes, it changes shape to fit the wielder's hand. Want to try?' Theo said, lifting it up towards her.

'It's okay,' she said, waving it away. 'Where's the blade?'

'I can summon it when I need it.'

'Show me.'

Theo wrapped his hand around the tail and lifted it up so that Mia could see it wiggle around as it molded itself perfectly to his hand.

'I'm not sure if that's sick or *sick*,' she said, the amazement clear in her eyes.

'You haven't seen anything yet.'

Theo activated the blade.

'Wow!' Mia said in genuine surprise as the slightly curved, slightly hooked blade appeared. 'So, it *is* all true. You used the medallion to pretend to be another cyclops, so you could fool the first one. But, how did I end up with two memories of the same day?'

'Well,' Theo paused for a moment while he decided whether to tell her or not. 'I can use the sword to travel through time and space.'

Mia was silent for a moment before saying in almost a whisper, 'No way. Can you show me?'

'Erm...' Theo said, suddenly realising he'd given too much away. 'It's not something to play with.'

'Why not? I would.'

'I shouldn't have shown you. Look, this isn't a toy,

it carries a lot of responsibility. Do you want to know why you remember two versions of the same day?'

Mia nodded.

'The snow one was what really happened. The first time around, I mean. I exposed my secret by saving everyone, so I travelled back in time and stopped the cyclops before we ever met him and that caused a time paradox.'

'A what?'

'A paradox. Two of me existed in the same time and place and that can't happen. Luckily the gods put it right for me. Or at least we thought they had. Somehow you still remember both versions of the same day.'

'The gods? Theo, this is sounding crazier by the second. What gods?'

'The ancient Greek gods,' Theo said.

Mia went quiet and Theo sat and stared at her for what felt like the length of a flight to Cyprus.

'You know what,' she said, 'I believe you. It's the only explanation, because if it's not, we're both going nuts.'

Theo looked at her. She wasn't freaking out and, more importantly, she looked like she believed him.

He opened the box of sandwiches and he told her.

Everything.

CHAPTER EIGHTEEN

Any doubts Theo had about sharing his secrets with Mia were gone by the time she went home. She'd stayed for tea in the end. He told her all about saving the world last year, the jar at the bottom of the ocean and the gorgon. But that wasn't all they'd talked about. They'd also talked about his dad.

He made sure Mia was out of the house before Mum got home though. Gran had teased him enough. There was no way he was giving Mum the opportunity. It would be a twenty-minute grilling about who she was, who her parents were and whether she had ever been in trouble at school or with the police.

That night, Theo lay in bed, the Sword of Chronos safely tucked away under his mattress once again. The Medallion was around his neck, as always, and the mirror was still hidden in the drawer. He'd checked it before he climbed in bed to see if Pappou had tried to contact him. He had, but Theo chose to ignore it. He decided to keep everything that happened a secret.

Theo's head hardly touched the pillow before he was asleep. The last few days and the extra time spent time-travelling, finally exhausting him.

When Theo awoke the next morning, his phone, which he had left charging next to his bed, was flashing blue. He picked it up and read the message. As he guessed, it was from Mia.

What are you up to today?

Theo smiled and sent back that he would let her know. It was Saturday, and Saturday was the one day Mum didn't work.

Unless there were exceptional circumstances.

He went downstairs in his pyjamas and entered the kitchen. Mum was getting breakfast ready. Theo had got used to his grandparents being there and it felt strange not having Gran busying herself and Granddad sitting at the breakfast bar reading the newspaper.

'Morning, Theo,' Mum said.

'Morning,' Theo mumbled back as he sat down and started looking through the breakfast cereals.

'I've been neglecting you — as usual. I've cleared my day, just for you. What do you want to do?'

'To be honest, I just fancy sitting around and not doing a lot. The holiday camp was exhausting.'

'It was an adventure camp, Theo. When you call it a holiday camp you make it sound like Butlins or something.'

Theo could tell just by the tone of her voice how she felt about Butlins. 'True. It wasn't much of a holiday, either.'

'What do you mean?' Again, her voice gave away her feelings. Theo had *definitely* said the wrong thing.

'It was great fun. It was just exhausting. We never stopped.'

'Good,' Mum said. 'Sounds like I got my money's worth.'

Theo nodded and poured some malted wheats into a bowl. 'What would you like to do today?' he said, trying to repair the situation a little.

'I'd like to do something with you,' she said, putting a glass of orange juice down in front of him.

What Theo really wanted to do was sit at home and watch films all day, but he knew his mum wouldn't be happy with that. He chose something he knew she'd love.

'Why don't we walk around the nature reserve and then have something to eat in the café?'

'That's a great idea. Finish your breakfast, then get going.'

The traffic was terrible and it took an hour rather than the usual twenty minutes to get to the nature reserve. It was such a nice day that everyone else must have had the same idea because it took them another fifteen minutes to find somewhere to park. Theo kept quiet as his mum got more and more exasperated as she went around and around the carpark.

The walk started off well enough and then Theo accidentally stood in some dog muck that some irresponsible owner hadn't picked up. Mum had a meltdown and suddenly it was Theo's fault for not looking where he was going.

They didn't have anything to eat in the cafe. Instead, they sat in silence for the whole drive home, the offending trainer in the boot of the car, wrapped up in three carrier bags to make sure the smell didn't escape. Theo wished he'd spent the day with Mia. At least he would have had fun. He wanted to text her, but, as usual, Mum had insisted he left his phone at home when they had 'quality time' together.

As soon they got home, Theo hopped into the house in his one trainer, kicked it off, not caring where it landed and ran upstairs. He was angry and frustrated with his mother, but he wasn't brave enough to slam his bedroom door. Instead, he threw himself onto the bed.

'Why? Why do you have to be like this, Mum?' he screamed into the pillow, fighting back the tears forming in the corners of his eyes.

Theo heard a gentle knock on the door and then it opened.

'I'm...I'm sorry,' Mum said.

Theo continued to bury his face in his pillow and listened as she crossed the bedroom floor. He felt the bed move as she sat down next to him. A part of him wanted to move away from her. Part of him wanted to move closer.

'I'm sorry,' she repeated.

'Gran's right. Why do you have to be so hard on me? About everything? All the time?' Theo said into the pillow.

'I...'

'Why didn't *you* die instead of Dad?'

The words were out of his mouth before he could stop them. Self-loathing crashed over him as the cruelty of his words sunk in. He quickly rolled over and looked at his mum. She was sat on the edge of the bed, staring at the carpet, like she was inspecting a new stain she'd just discovered.

'How could you say that?' she said, turning to face him. Tears were streaming down her face.

'I'm sorry. I didn't mean it. I...' The words died in Theo's mouth. It was too late. What was said could never be unsaid.

'I don't mean to be hard on you,' Mum said. 'It's...it's hard on my own. I have to be a Mum *and* a Dad. And I have to rely on Pamela and Roger so much. I know I don't spend enough time with you, but...' Mum stopped for a moment and a smile appeared on her face even though she was still crying. 'But, you look so much like him. And I miss him too, Theo. I miss him too.'

Theo threw himself into his mother's arms and they sobbed together for the first time in the four years that Dad had been gone.

They cried and cried until they both feel asleep, exhausted.

CHAPTER NINETEEN

Theo awoke. It was dark outside and his mother was no longer on the bed next to him. As silently as he could, he left his bedroom and went to his mother's room. The door was closed, as usual. Theo slowly turned the handle and pushed the door open. It brushed against the carpet, making a sound that seemed as loud as a thunder storm in the otherwise quiet room.

Mum was asleep, lying on her side and facing the window. The curtains were open so the early morning light would wake her up and she could begin catching up on the work she hadn't done while she had spent the day with him.

For the first time in Theo's life he didn't resent it. In all the years since it had been just him and his mum he had never given a thought about how she might be feeling. He'd been deeply selfish. Of course she was hurting. He was, so why wouldn't she?

Closing the door quietly behind him, Theo went crept back to his own room and gathered the mirror, the sword and his usual backpack. Opening a portal, he mouthed 'I love you' in his mother's direction and stepped through.

Cyprus was two hours ahead of England and the sky above Mount Olympus was bright with the light of a new day.

Theo stood by the side of the road, looking at the place where his father had been knocked off his motorbike. He wished he'd brought flowers with him. Every year he came up here with Mum and Pappou and they placed flowers on the ground where he was standing right now. The first year Gran and Granddad came. There was plans for everyone to come next year when it was the fifth anniversary of Dad's death.

Now that he was thinking about it all properly for the first time ever, Theo realised why it was the three of them who came here. After a few minutes Pappou would guide Theo away and leave Mum alone. Pappou would distract him by pointing out the local landmarks. You could see Aphrodite's Rock, of course, but Theo had always been more fascinated by the huge radar domes the British government had built there as part of RAF Troodos.

Theo took a deep breath and closed his eyes. 'Dad, if you can hear me, I need your advice.' His words were lifted up by the early morning breeze and carried away.

Theo shook his head. What was he thinking? Was he so used to hearing voices in his head now that he expected his dad to answer? That wasn't it. He'd talked to Dad loads of times, just always in his head.

His father always had good advice. For someone who lived a life of action as a firefighter, he was a very good listener. Theo smiled. Maybe that was why he got on so well with Mum. She was a talker.

'Dad,' Theo said, starting again. 'I have this power, I can travel through time. I can come back and save you. I can...I can save Mum from being—' Theo choked on his own guilt, unable to say the words 'unhappy and lonely'.

'But if I do, everything will change. Something terrible might happen. I'm so confused. I don't know what to do. Help me?'

A tear rolled down Theo's cheek and he took a step back and sat on the rock he and Calista had sat on the last time he'd been there. He looked down at the Sword of Chronos in his hands, his knuckles white from gripping it so hard.

'Theo?'

At first he wasn't sure he'd heard the voice or not, then he turned and looked over his shoulder.

Calista stood a few paces away.

'Are you okay?' she asked, moving closer.

Theo wiped the back of his hand across his face,

smearing the tears rather than hiding them like he intended. 'I'm fine.'

'You don't look fine.'

Calista sat beside him. Theo could feel her looking at him, but he didn't speak.

'Why?' he eventually said.

'Why what?' Calista said, looking confused.

'Why do I have all these gifts,' he said lifting up the hand that held the sword 'only to be told I can't even use them to help myself. To make my own life better.'

Calista put a hand on his shoulder. 'Because, Theo, that is the path of a hero. The test. A hero must sacrifice himself for others. For the greater good. He must leave behind his own wants and desires.'

Theo turned and looked at her, tears in his eyes. 'Who made these rules? Who decided this?'

'You must, if you want to be a hero.'

'Do I have a choice? I didn't name myself Kyrios ton Pithon. What if I don't want to be a hero?'

'Some of the burdens you carry were already with you before you became the Lord of the Vases, do not forget that.'

'When did you get so wise?' Theo said, glancing across at Calista. For a moment she appeared different, her skin around her eyes wrinkled. It must have been the tears clouding his eyes. He rubbed his eyes and had another look. This time she looked like her usual twelve-year-old self.

'Theo, I am wise because I have seen everything

this world has to offer. The good and the bad. The happy and the sad.'

'You're only twelve, what do you know?' Theo said, hearing his own bitterness. 'Have you lost a mum or dad?'

'Calista is twelve, and no, she has not been as unfortunate as you. But I have lost many, many people that I love.'

Theo looked up at her. Why was she referring to herself in the third person?

'You wanted to know who I am — what I am? I am...' Calista paused and smiled. 'It's funny, I have never explained it before and although I know almost every word in almost every human language that exists, or has ever existed, I cannot find the right ones.'

'You sound different. I can't explain how, but you do. It's like… you don't sound like a kid anymore. You haven't for the last few minutes.'

Calista smiled and Theo was certain her face changed again, this time to look like a younger version of herself, like she was five or six years old.

'What's going on?' Theo cried, scrambling to his feet, suddenly afraid.

'Theo, the time has come for me to show you my true self. The time for games is over. I am twelve, just like you. But I am also older. Much older.'

Theo had seen so many amazing things over the last twelve months that he thought nothing could surprise him anymore, but he was wrong. Before his eyes Calista's face began to change. And it kept changing, getting younger, older and then somewhere in between. It was like a collection of photos of Calista at different ages with pictures of her gran, aunt and sister mixed in.

'What are you?' Theo said, stumbling back.

'I am here to support and guide you through your toughest challenges, just as I helped Theseus all those years ago. I am of the bloodline of Ariadne, and like you, I have a gift. But mine is different. Within me I have Ariadne's undying soul. I *am* Calista, but I am also a vessel for Ariadne, just as the vases in the Hall of Heroes hold the heroes' souls or the Hall holds Oracle.'

'I…understand,' Theo said, putting his hand down on the rock and steadying himself. 'I think. So, are you three thousand years old?'

'Calista isn't, but Ariadne is. Right now, Calista has given her body over to me. Right now, you are talking to Ariadne. That is why I sound different.'

'So, what should I call you?'

'Calista,' she said, smiling. 'I am always Calista.'

'I'm confused,' Theo said, sitting down again and rubbing his head.

'I have decided to reveal the truth about myself to you because the time is coming. The time of the test.'

'Test?'

'The reason why you are Kyrios ton Pithon.'

'But that was the eclipse last year. The escape of the minotaur and putting everything back the way it should be.'

'No, Theo, that was but the beginning. The forces of darkness are growing. Their agents are reaching out and soon The Net will be ripped apart, unless we do something about it. '

'We?'

'Yes. You are not alone. The Guardians have never been alone. *You* have never been alone.'

'But, Pappou doesn't trust you.'

Calista laughed. 'That can be easily solved. Come,' she said, taking his hand, 'we must go to the Hall.'

Theo nodded his head, stood up and extended the blade on the Sword of Chronos.

'Don't worry, we don't need that today,' Calista said.

Theo felt his body tingle all over, and then everything went black.

CHAPTER TWENTY

Theo's back was cold, and it felt like a satyr was dancing on his head. He was in the dark. An alarm was sounding, and someone was shouting at him. It felt like his head was full of sawdust and cotton wool and he couldn't make out who was speaking or what was being said.

'Intruder. Intruder. Intruder,' the voice blared, over and over again.

Theo sat up. His head swam.

'It's me, Oracle,' he said, recognising the voice at last. 'Turn off the alarm, there's no intruder.'

The alarm fell silent, but Oracle continued to talk. 'Negative, One-Hundred. There is someone with you. You both appeared without the use of the Sword of Chronos. That should not have been allowed.'

'She's with me,' Theo called through the darkness. 'Calista? Are you okay?'

'I'm over here,' Calista replied from the darkness. 'Sorry. I didn't mean to alarm your toy.'

'Excuse me?' Oracle said. 'I am *not* a toy. I'll have you know—'

'Yes, yes, I know,' Calista said, cutting her off. 'You're the living spirit of the Pythia, the ancient Oracle of Delphi. You are able to communicate directly to the gods and as such, have a vast, almost limitless amount of knowledge as well as your own skills of organisation, deduction and imagination.'

'How do you know that? They are exactly the words Pythagoras used to describe me when he visited here. Do I know you?' Oracle asked.

'You've met *half* of me before,' Calista replied from the gloom.

'Half?'

'Can we please have some lights on,' Calista said, ignoring Oracle's question.

'Good idea,' Theo said, clicking his fingers. The torches flickered on, one at a time, filling the Hall of Heroes with light.

'How did we get here? I feel terrible,' Theo said, putting his hand to his head and walking over to Calista, who was stood next to the temple table.

'Sorry. I should have warned you. I can travel using a much quicker and convenient way than your sword. As you've discovered, it does come with side-effects. You get used to it — sort of.'

'Would someone mind telling me what is going on

here?' Oracle said, sounding even more snooty than usual. 'How can I know half of you?'

'Oracle, thi—' Theo began.

'I'm Calista,' she said stepping up to the Olympus table and placing her hands onto its cool surface. And it was her, too. Theo could tell she was now back in control and not the calmer, more thoughtful, Ariadne.

'Please remove your hands,' Oracle said.

'Make me,' Calista challenged her.

Theo rolled his eyes and stood at Calista's side. 'Can't we just get along and play nicely?'

'*She* is rude,' Oracle announced.

'She—' Calista began.

Theo slapped his hand down on the table. It stung and didn't make the loud noise he was hoping it would, but it did stop Calista talking.

For a moment.

'All right, calm down,' she said, shaking her head at him.

'Calista, why don't you introduce yourself?'

'There is no need. I have worked out who she is. You should not have touched the table, young lady, if you wanted me to take longer to figure it out,' Oracle said. 'One Hundred, Ninety-Eight will not be impressed you have let her in here. We have had dealings with *her* before.'

'Actually, *I've* never been in here,' Calista said, as she stepped to the side and started to remove books from the columns at the corners of the temple table.

'You, Calista, have not been here before, no, but

your grandmother, Cipriana, was banned after what she did.'

'Banned? Sounds exciting,' Calista said, as she circled the table, running her fingers along its smooth surface. 'Tell me, Oracle, what did my grandmother do that got your knickers in such a twist? No, hang on, I can find out for myself.' Calista put her fingers on her temples and rubbed her head the way she had when she remembered how Tomb 6A had changed.

'One hundred,' Oracle said. 'I must warn you that we have not had anything to do with this girl's family since the *incident*. I am going to contact Ninety-Eight. He needs to know what is going on here.'

'Tell him I'll open a portal for him in his kitchen so he doesn't have to swim here.'

'Very well,' Oracle answered.

Calista let out a sharp, sudden laugh. Theo turned to look at her, confused by her sudden outburst.

'That was funny,' Calista said.

'What was?' Theo asked, confused.

'No, it was not,' Oracle replied.

'Will you stop having your own conversation and include me on what's going on here?' Theo said, his frustration growing.

'I'll tell you later, you'll love this 'incident' she's talking about. Looks to me that Oracle and your grandfather just need to get a sense of humour.'

Theo groaned. He didn't want to know. He didn't want to be dragged into their argument. He was getting tired of it already and when Pappou arrived, all Tartarus would break loose. At least when Pappou complained to him he could genuinely say he hadn't brought her here.

'Theo, put the sword away, I can get Oracle's master for you,' Calista said, in a helpful tone of voice, though Theo could tell she was being anything but.

'Ninety-Eight is *not* my master.'

'Of course not, Oracle,' Calista said with a wicked grin. 'Theo is, or should I call him Kyrios ton Pithon. Don't you think you should call him that, rather just plain old One-Hundred?'

Theo sighed. He'd had enough. 'Will you two please stop it. Can I trust you to get along if I leave you here while I go and get Pappou?'

'That won't be necessary.' Pappou's deep voice echoed from the tunnel as he emerged from its dark mouth. 'I had a bad feeling when I woke up this morning and decided to come. It's a good job I did. Theo, why did you bring her here? And where were you yesterday? I was trying to contact you all day. We have a mystery to solve with a very high price, or have you forgotten?' Pappou removed his oxygen tank and put it out of the way by the chest.

'I'm sorry I—'

'You don't need to tell Theo off. He didn't bring me here,' Calista said over the top of him. 'I brought *him*.'

'How did you get through the shield?' Pappou asked as he approached the table.

'We've already been over this,' Calista said, rolling her eyes, 'with her ladyship.'

'And, Ninety-Eight, she did not give an acceptable answer,' Oracle said.

'It's simple really,' Calista said. 'I've been here before, or at least my grandmother has, therefore I can find my way back in. It's not really that hard to understand. I am basically the same as Oracle except Ariadne gets to live inside me, rather than a cold, dark cave. It's no wonder Oracle's grumpy all the time. You could at least install some heating.'

'I am *not* grumpy.'

'Right!' Pappou said, barely holding in his temper. 'I've only been here a few seconds and I'm already sick of the pair of you. Behave or leave,' Pappou said to Calista, pointing a shaking finger at her. It moved onto the next person he was talking to. 'Oracle, use some of that fabled patience and wisdom you're supposed to have. The girl is just winding you up. Theo?' Again, the finger moved. 'With me. Now.'

Pappou turned and walked back to the tunnel. Theo quietly followed behind him.

'What on earth do you think you're doing?' Pappou asked as soon as they were out of sight.

'*I* didn't bring her here. She grabbed my hand and *she* brought us here!'

'I can still hear you!' Calista called from around the corner.

Pappou grabbed Theo's hand and led him further down the tunnel.

'We don't work with them anymore,' he said.

'So, what she says is true, she is the Bloodline of Ariadne?'

'Yes, but we don't work with them anymore,' Pappou repeated.

'Why not?'

'Because of the way they behave.'

'I know they're two souls in one body, but can you please call her Calista?'

'I warned you not to have anything to do with her last year. You let her see the mirror and—'

'We're meant to be a team,' Theo interrupted. 'She helped Theseus all those years ago and she helped me when I was on Crete, too. I would have been lost in the maze without her.'

'Not true. Oracle guided you through it with Daedalus' plans. And that's beside the point. We haven't had anything to do with them for the last two generations. They...' Pappou stopped.

'What, Pappou?'

'They…' Pappou paused. 'They are unreliable.'

'What he's trying to say,' said Calista — she was suddenly standing right next to them — 'is that over time, the bond between the soul of Ariadne and the host body, me in this case, has become...'

'Unstable. There you go, I said it,' Pappou blurted.

'What do you mean, "unstable"?' Theo asked.

'He's trying to be polite. He means mad,' Calista said. 'He thinks I'm mad.'

'I never said that. I meant that you are...unpredictable,' Pappou said, looking pleased with his choice of word. 'That's it. Unpredictable.'

'Come on, Xever, that's what makes me interesting,' Calista said.

'Interesting is certainly one word for it. And I didn't give you permission to call me Xever.'

'Right,' Theo said, determinedly. He was sick of this. 'I'm in charge here, agreed?'

'You are Kyrios ton Pithon,' Oracle said from around the corner.

'Now you decide to join in,' Pappou said. 'Thanks for the support.'

'Pappou, Calista, I'm in charge here, so I'm ordering you all — you too, Oracle — to stop this. We've got work to do. From now on we're a team. Got it?'

Pappou's shoulders slumped. Calista smiled.

'Right, follow me.' Theo led them back into the cave and up to the table.

Everyone spread out, picking a side of the table each. Theo felt strange not standing next to his grandfather, but he was a leader now and that would have to be one of the sacrifices.

'Calista, have you managed to find out anything about that coin I gave you?' Theo asked.

'You gave her the—' Pappou began, but Theo silenced him by putting up his finger.

'I do have something, yes,' Calista said.

Theo looked at her and noticed her smile had gone.

CHAPTER TWENTY-ONE

'Calista, tell us what you've found,' Theo said.

'Okay,' she said, taking a deep breath. 'To be honest, I recognised the coin straight away. It was why I wanted to take it off you.'

Theo wanted to ask her why she hadn't told him at the time but knew it would only start arguments again.

'When I say "I", I, of course, mean Ariadne. As I'm sure you know, Theo, The Net was not constructed straight away when the Bloodline of Theseus and Ariadne began their mission.'

'I've not had a chance to give him the full history, yet,' Pappou said, a little defensively.

'I'm sure you've been very busy,' Calista said, politely.

Now that Theo thought about it, he didn't really know much at all about the Guardians, their history or their rules and regulations. He had only ever been told enough to achieve what was needed.

'The Net was created by the gods in the final days of their powers, before other religions came along and became more popular,' Calista said.

'And they wiped mankind's minds so we would think they, and all the beasts and heroes, were just stories. I do know that much,' Theo said.

'That's right,' Calista continued. 'Remember how we were talking about Theseus leaving me, or rather Ariadne, on the island?'

'Yes, of course. We discussed which was the true story.'

'The answer is neither. Zeus visited Theseus and Ariadne on board their ship and told them of the mission he had in mind for them. He knew that the power of the gods would one day wane and so sent them both on a mission to build this Hall of Heroes.'

'Then why didn't he visit me? I was the one on the boat, not Theseus.'

'He's a god, Theo. He knew you weren't really Theseus,'

'This is all very interesting,' Oracle said, 'but what does it have to do with the coin?'

'I'm getting to it, if you'll let me,' said Calista.

Theo gave her a warning look.

'Theseus and Ariadne began their mission wandering the lands of Greece, doing heroic deeds blah blah blah. Occasionally we teamed up, but we kept it hush hush — I was married to Dionysus and he is a jealous god underneath all that partying. Well, one of my solo missions brought me into contact with Arachne — *the* Arachne, from the weaving story. I came across her hidden in a cave.'

'Caves, why does it always have to be caves?' Theo muttered.

'Around her she had gathered all sorts of weaving equipment, but instead of making beautiful fabric on her loom, she retreated into the caves, spinning webs instead.'

'So, this cave? Where is it?' Theo asked, hoping to hurry Calista along.

'In the mountains on the island of Zakynthos.'

'Isn't that where Apollo and Artemis lived?' Theo said.

Pappou reached over and squeezed Theo's shoulder, like he did whenever Theo remembered his Greek mythology. Pappou hadn't told him all about the workings of the Guardians, but he had made sure Theo knew his history.

'Exactly. I met Artemis once,' Calista said, 'Or rather one of my bloodline did. She was very nice. And a great teacher. And boy, could she use a bow and arrow.'

'So, you know where Arachne lived. Have you been to see if she's still there?' asked Pappou.

'I have.'

'And?' asked Theo.

'Sadly, she wasn't there.'

'Great, all that explaining for nothing,' Theo said, frustrated.

'She wasn't there, at that time, but she had been. It's a place to start.'

'True,' Pappou said. 'Can you tell us the exact location?'

'I can do better than that. I'll take you there. Remember I can travel to any place I've been to before.'

'You two go,' Pappou said. 'I'll man the fort here with Oracle. Do you have everything you need?'

Theo patted the backpack behind him. 'I never leave home without it.'

'Me neither,' Pappou said, unzipping his wetsuit and pulling out the other Mirror of Aphrodite.

'Lovely,' said Calista. 'I'm sure the goddess of love and beauty loves being stuffed in there.'

To Theo's amazement, Pappou said nothing. He even smiled.

'Right, hold my hand hero, it's time the Bloodlines of Ariadne and Theseus worked together once again,' said Calista.

'Just give me some warning before we teleport, or whatever it is you do,' Theo said, taking her hand.

'Of course. Make sure you stay on your feet this time.'

'What do you mean?'

Theo felt the tingling sensation come over his body, the urge to be sick and then everything went black.

The next thing Theo could see was dazzling light. He threw his arm up to cover his face. Wherever they were, he was staring right into the sun.

'It's a great view, when your eyes get used to it,' Calista said.

Theo lowered his eyes to avoid the glare and immediately wished he hadn't.

'What the...!' Theo cried and threw his body back even though he didn't know what was behind him. Right then it didn't matter. All that mattered was the sheer drop right in front of his toes. Theo gripped Calista's hand and went back to staring at the bright blue sky.

'You could have warned me!' he cried, risking another glance. He still couldn't believe where they were. They were balanced on a narrow outcropping of rock on a cliff, just wide enough for their feet to fit on.

'I thought it was best if I didn't. You might not have wanted to come. I did warn you to stay on your feet.'

Theo looked at Calista. What had Pappou said about her being unstable? Was this her idea of a joke? Did she find this fun?

'This is madness, you could have killed us. I'm sick of caves… and cliffs,' Theo said. He'd always been afraid of heights, but he'd thought he'd got over it when he'd climbed down the trellis at King Aegeus' palace. Maybe he still had some work to do.

'Look, we're here now. I got us as close as I could. I

couldn't risk teleporting us into the cave in case she's there and we were spotted by her or someone else.'

'Thanks for the consideration. How did Arachne get up here? If she's as big as her offspring, she could never walk along this.'

'Think about it, Theo. You're a clever boy. Come on, this way.'

Theo suddenly realised he was still holding her hand. He let go and followed her along the shelf of rock, shuffling his feet one at a time.

The heat from the sun was fierce, but the stiff breeze kept it a tolerable temperature. Suddenly Theo had an extra worry. What if a strong gust of wind plucked him off the shelf? How far down was it? He didn't dare look. He kept his eyes locked onto the back of Calista's head as he continued to shuffle along the shelf.

'Look, it's just a little further. Be careful though, this is where the shelf gets narrower,' Calista called as she speeded up and moved further away from him.

Theo continued to nudge himself along a little at a time. Sweat beaded across his brow and it wasn't all because of the heat. He was living out his worst nightmare.

Suddenly his toes tipped forward over the edge. It was only the tiniest amount, but it felt like a ninety-degree change. He wobbled for a moment, his heart and breathing stopping for an instant. The wind suddenly picked up and Theo was sure he was going to be plucked off the side of the cliff.

'I'm...I'm not sure I can do this,' he said between short, sharp breaths.

'Keep going, we're almost there.'

Theo moved his foot along. It felt like a large step, but he suspected it was probably mere millimetres.

'I'm at the cave,' Calista called.

Theo wanted to look at her, to see how far it was, but he couldn't. His eyes stayed fixed straight ahead, staring at the clear blue sky.

'Theo, I'm reaching out for you.'

He closed his eyes for a moment and then forced his head to turn and look. Calista's fingers were just out of reach.

'Come on. You can do it,' Calista urged, her voice surprisingly encouraging.

Theo stretched and felt his fingertips touch hers.

'I did it,' he said, confidence blooming inside him.

That was when the shelf decided to crumble beneath him.

CHAPTER TWENTY-TWO

Theo plummeted from the tiny ledge like a sky-diver, face down, his arms and legs thrashing about in terror. He would have been staring at his doom if he hadn't closed his eyes.

Theo! screamed Theseus. *You* need *to look.*

Theo ignored the hero's cry and kept his eyes firmly shut.

Maybe dying wouldn't be so bad. Perhaps he would get to see Dad again.

But then Mum will have lost us both, Theo thought. *And she'll never find me or find out how it happened.*

Open. Your. Eyes, Theseus yelled inside Theo's head.

This time, Theo did as he was commanded. Not just because of the command, but at the thought of his heartbroken mother. He had just started to fix things with her. He couldn't leave the healing unfinished.

The first thing he saw was the grey rock blurring

past him. He didn't dare look down. Knowing how much time he had — or how little — would be of no help. He needed an idea and fast. What was it that Calista had just said about how Arachne had got here?

Of course!

Theo closed his eyes again, but this time it was to help him focus. As usual, Theo didn't feel anything change, but he knew the Medallion of Morpheus had worked its magic.

He opened his eyes and looked at the huge, round spider body beneath him and his own sticking out of the top of it.

It was time to stop his descent.

And now he had eight legs, it should be easy.

If he could work out how to move them.

See it in your mind, like you did before, Theseus said. *Reach out with them. Now! Do it now!*

Theo looked at the hairy legs and willed them to move. Barely a second after thinking it, the legs reached out and brushed against the hard rock.

And skidded along its rough surface.

He cried in pain as it seared through the tip of each leg, forcing them to flinch away. As his yell was carried away by the wind, he felt a strange, tingling sensation in various places in his body. Four separate streams of silk burst from spinnerets at the end of his spider body. The shining ropes joined as one and latched onto the wall. He fell for a second longer and then the silk slowed his descent until he came to a stop.

Theo reached out with his legs, their ends still tender, and stopped himself from smashing into the cliff face. Once he was sure they had a firm grip on the rock, Theo looked down and swallowed between heaving breaths. The rock-strewn ground at the base of the cliff was just a few metres below him. Thank goodness something had set off the spinnerets!

Theo looked up at the looming cliff in front of him. He wasn't sure how far up it was — at least the length of three swimming pools, he guessed — but there was no sign of Calista. Perhaps she thought he hadn't made it.

Theo imagined the silk detaching itself from his body and it swung away, caught in the breeze that came around the mountain. Flexing his spider legs, Theo walked up the sheer rockface. The eight limbs worked as a well-timed team, their tiny hairs gripping the surface. Theo found he had a new appreciation for the terrible creatures that lurked in the corner of his bedroom.

'Calista?!' he called as he neared the top.

'Hurry up, will you. It's getting cold waiting up here,' she shouted. Her face appeared briefly before she sat down, her legs dangling over the edge, reminding Theo of the time she had done the exact same thing at Tomb 6A.

'I'm coming as fast as I can. I almost died, Calista! Thanks for your help, by the way.'

Calista shrugged. 'I knew you could handle it. The cave mouth's right behind me. Once you get up here, there's plenty of room for you and your enormous bottom.' She moved out of the way as Theo climbed up over the edge.

As soon as Theo was at the cave mouth, he changed back to himself. He turned and looked back out at the blue sky. The cave entrance was the perfect hiding place for a giant spider. It was almost impossible to get to without the right climbing equipment, guts and nerves of steel.

'Ready to go inside?' Calista asked.

Theo nodded, unable to speak for a moment. It really had been a close call. He took off his backpack and took out the Sword of Chronos. 'Let's be prepared. You said you've been here before. Ladies first?'

The cave grew smaller and darker as they walked further in. Theo felt like the sides were pressing in on him.

'I thought you said you found her weaving equipment?' Theo said, looking around at the empty cave. 'Where is it? Has someone beaten us to it?'

'You know, if you asked less questions at once I could answer them more easily,' Calista said, stepping to the side so that the light from outside lit up the back of the cave.

Theo surveyed the rock surface and noticed a dark shadow in the corner. Stepping closer, he found it wasn't what he first assumed it was, but an opening in the rock, just large enough for Arachne to have climbed through.

'It took me a while to find it too. It was disguised once upon a time. When we're through, we'll need your sword to see,' Calista said as she got down on the cold, hard floor.

Theo extended the blade in his hand. 'I really need to bring a torch. Making this glow requires effort, you know.'

'Stop whingeing,' Calista said as she entered the opening. A few moments later she called to let him know she was through.

Theo squatted down and tried to look through the opening and into the darkness beyond. It was impossible. 'Here we go,' he muttered and eased his way through the gap.

'Be careful what you touch,' Calista said, her voice echoing slightly.

Theo almost didn't hear her, he was so engrossed by what he saw. The small cavern in front of him was both beautiful and frightening. The loom and other weaving equipment were there, just as Calista had said. What she hadn't included was how everything was encased in cobwebs and spider-silk. It was so thick in places, the room looked like it was covered in a blanket of snow.

'What now?' Theo asked.

'Look, some candles,' Calista said, picking one up from the top of a crate and rubbing stray bits of webbing off it. The candle was huge, wide enough that her fingers didn't wrap all the way around it.

'Great, all we need now is a way of lighting it,' Theo said.

'She needed a way to light them, so there must be something, somewhere,' Calista said, putting the candle down on the web-covered crate and rooting around. 'Here,' she said, picking up an old knife and a stone. 'Flint and steel.'

She bundled up a collection of webs and placed them on a clear patch on the floor in front of them. With the flint in one hand and the knife in the other, she struck them together, creating sparks. One landed on the webbing and it began to burn. Grabbing the candle, she dipped the wick into the flames. It's flickering yellow light joined the aura from Theo's sword.

'Where next?' Theo asked.

'We'll explore a little deeper. Clearly, she's not here, and neither are her children.'

'You're the detective, lead the way.'

Calista held the candle higher and began to follow the path through the cave. The light reflected off the whiteness that covered all the objects down either side. Theo had no idea what lay beneath it.

'Theo, through here,' Calista said.

He had just enough time to see her cup her hand around the flame of the candle before she disappeared through a gap in the wall.

'I'm through,' Calista called, her voice rapidly followed by an echo.

Theo stepped into the opening and felt the rush of air that had caused Calista to protect her flame. When he emerged from the other side, the light from the candle and the Sword of Chronos, lit up the area around them, but nothing more. It didn't reflect off any walls or any equipment.

'How big is this place?' Theo said. A moment later he heard his voice echo back at him.

'It must be massive. Come on.'

They continued walking, their footsteps echoing off the walls. The distorted noises made Theo's flesh crawl. What if someone, or something, was in there with them. He looked around nervously — up, down, left, right — but it was just too dark to see.

'Look,' Calista said, pointing at something white on the edge of their circle of light.

'More cobwebs?' Theo asked.

'I don't know. It looks a little different. Let's take a closer look.'

'What *are* they?' Theo asked as they got nearer.

A collection of five orbs of spider silk lay snuggled up around the bones of what once had been a goat, a sheep or perhaps a calf. Theo leaned a little closer. The top of each sphere had been ripped open. From the inside.

'I think they're spider eggs,' said Calista. 'Or should that be arachne eggs?'

'That's what I was afraid you'd say.'

'Theo,' Calista said with a wonky smile and a sparkle in her eyes. 'Are you afraid of spiders?'

'No, not exactly. But if there's eggs and they've hatched…' Theo turned and looked around, waving his sword into the darkness. Maybe it hadn't just been a feeling after all and someone *was* watching them.

'Can't you make that thing any brighter?' Calista said, nodding towards the sword.

'Why? Are *you* scared?'

'Just do it.'

Theo gripped the sword tighter and muttered the incantation under his breath. The blade grew a little brighter.

'Wow!' Calista said, her voice quiet and whispery. 'They're everywhere.'

Scattered around them in small piles were eggs. Hundreds of eggs.

'Great!' Theo muttered.

'What's that?' Calista pointed at something else at the edge of the light.

Whatever it was, Theo had a bad feeling about it. A very bad feeling.

CHAPTER TWENTY-THREE

Theo loosened his grip on the hilt of the Sword of Chronos and its blade dimmed until it no longer glowed.

'What is it?' he asked as he stepped up to Calista, glad of the light from her candle.

'You said the arachne kidnapped the centaur children?'

'Yes. Why?'

'Do you have the mirror with you?' Calista asked.

'Of course. It's in my backpack.' Theo turned to allow her to unzip it and reach inside.

'Xever? Oracle?' Calista said into the mirror's face.

'You're not holding it right. Look, you need to put your thumb here,' Theo said adjusting the position of her hand.

The face of the mirror took on a gentle, green glow and Pappou appeared. He had a thick book out on the top of the table and he was staring intently at it as he flicked through the pages. 'Yes, Theo, what is it?'

'I'm afraid it's me, Calista.'

'Oh,' Pappou said, his tone short before it suddenly took on an entirely different one. 'He's not hurt, is he?'

'Of course not. You can trust me,' Calista said, smiling.

Pappou responded with the usual 'Hmmmmmm' he saved for when he didn't want to give an answer.

'Don't worry, I'm right here, Pappou,' Theo said, grabbing Calista's hand and twisting it so the mirror faced him.

'How can we help you?' said Oracle.

'I'm not sure if what I'm going to suggest is possible, Oracle,' Calista said, adjusting the angle of the mirror so both she and Theo were in it like they were taking a selfie. 'But can you use the mirror to scan the area ahead of us?'

'It has never been tried,' Oracle said. 'But I cannot see why not. As long as I can see what you are seeing via the mirror then I can do the scan.'

'That's what I was hoping. I need a temporal scan of the area in front of us. Can you show us what you detect rather than just telling us?'

'I might be able to project a hologram through the mirror so that you can see it as well.'

'That would be perfect.'

'Please rotate the mirror to face what you wish me to scan,' Oracle said.

Calista did as Oracle asked.

'One moment, please.'

'I would never have thought of that,' Theo said.

Calista opened her mouth to say something and shut it again, leaving Theo curious about what she was going to say. He suspected it probably wasn't something nice. She'd obviously used her daily allowance of politeness on Oracle.

'Interesting,' Oracle said. 'And upsetting.'

Theo heard Pappou make a short intake of breath and say, 'Oh my goodness.'

'What? What is it?' Theo asked.

A moment later a beam of blue light burst from the head of the mirror creating a hologram. The glowing image perfectly overlapped the wooden fencing in front of them and flooded the cave with light, finally giving them some idea of how large the cave was.

Five centaur children lay on the straw, chains and manacles fastened around each of their four ankles.

'It's what I was afraid of,' Calista said.

Theo turned and looked at her. Her voice sounded gentle, serious even. He put his hand on her shoulder half-expecting her to shrug it off. She didn't.

'Why were they invisible before?' Theo asked.

'They weren't. Oracle's looking into the past and showing us what *was* here.'

'Of course,' Theo said, feeling a little foolish. 'Oracle, when in time are we looking?'

'This temporal image is from two hundred years ago.'

'Two hundred? I guess it was so they could hide here,' Theo suggested.

'Wait. There is more,' Oracle said. 'I am picking something up...something from twenty years after these images.'

'What is it?' Theo asked.

'Kyrios ton Pithon, forgive me, I am afraid that something is interfering with my scan and—'

The light of the hologram winked out, leaving only the flickering candle illumining the area.

'Pappou? Are you there?' Theo said, taking the mirror from Calista's hand. The mirror's face has returned to its lifeless polished bronze. The signal had been cut.

'Did you change your grip?' Theo asked, trying not to panic. 'Did you disconnect the call?'

'I don't know,' Calista said.

Theo could tell by the look on her face she was worried too. 'He wouldn't have cut us off. Something must have happened.'

'Try calling again.'

Theo gripped the mirror, but nothing happened.

'We should go back to the Hall of Heroes, they might need us,' he said.

'Maybe.'

'Maybe?' Theo said, shocked at Calista's answer. 'You might not care, but Pappou, Oracle and I are a team. We—'

'I know Theo, but I think they're okay. Think about it. Oracle said something was interfering with her scan. What if it was that *something* that cut them off? What if that something is trying to stop us finding something out? Oracle also mentioned an event that happened twenty years later. One hundred and eighty years ago. Perhaps we should go back and find out what that was.'

'It could be anything. We could walk into a trap,' Theo answered.

'We could, but we're heroes, remember?'

'Okay,' Theo said, nodding. 'Let's follow this lead. As soon as I create the portal, jump through and I'll follow.'

'Wait—' Calista said, but it was too late, Theo brought the sword down and opened the portal. He pushed her on the back, sending her through, and quickly followed her.

Theo didn't notice the portal snap shut behind him, but he did feel Calista grab his shoulder and force him down behind the wooden fence.

'What?!' he snapped.

'Shhhhhh!' Calista said, a finger to her lips. 'I was going to say we should find a safe place to open the portal first, in case anyone saw us coming.'

'Sorry,' Theo mouthed back. He hadn't thought about that. The cave might have been empty when they were before, but what about now, one hundred and eighty years earlier?

'Everything seems okay. Listen. There's no alarm going off or shouting warriors. Shall we look?'

Theo nodded. They slowly poked their heads over

the top of the fence, which was now complete and in good repair. The whole cave was lit up — there were candles just like the one Calista held everywhere — and for the first time they could see around them.

Aside from the pen, which was littered with fresh straw, but empty of centaurs, there were no other structures. Theo assumed Arachne and her children didn't need homes to sleep in. Perhaps they just hung off the walls or gathered in corners of the cavern.

'Where is everyone? Maybe we're too late,' she whispered.

Theo shrugged just as a horn sounded to their left.

'Look!' Calista said. 'Over there.'

Theo quickly took in what she was pointing out and ducked down out of sight. Calista remained exactly where she was. He bobbed back up next to her, his eyes just above the fence. The pen they were in was right at the edge of the cave. About twenty metres away at the centre was a gathering of what he thought were humans. But as he looked closer, he saw they were humans with animals for their lower halves — and not just spiders. There were centaurs too, standing side by side with the arachne. Both races had weapons in their hands, and they weren't pointing them at each other.

'What's going on? Why aren't they fighting? They look like they're…friends,' Theo said, as he watched a centaur and an arachne stand beside each other, talking and slapping each other playfully on the back.

'I don't know, but I bet it's not good.'

'Where's Arachne herself?'

'I can't see her anywh— Wait. There,' Calista said, pointing upwards with her chin.

Arachne lowered herself down on a piece of spider-silk from the top of the cavern until she hung above the gathered band of warriors.

Her hair was long and braided with streaks of white in it. Theo wondered if they were grey hairs or strands of spider silk. Her body was covered in a bronze chest plate, its surface decorated with a stylised web. Over her human shoulder, Theo could see the handle of a sword. Despite her red eyes, which glowed ever so slightly, she had a beautiful face.

'My children,' she said, her words echoing around the cavern. 'The time has come for us to carry out the last stage of our plan. When it is complete I — *we* — shall be free. It is time to punish the families that abandoned you, my adopted children.'

The gathered centaurs raised their weapons into the air and cheered.

'Of course,' Theo said, realising. 'Twenty years. The centaur children have grown up. But...they weren't abandoned, Arachne's army stole them. What's going on?'

'Shhh!' Calista said, putting her finger to her lips.

'Our leader will be joining us on this mission for revenge. At last, Chiron will get what he deserves, and if our leader's plan is as foolproof as she claims, so will the boy. Once again our kind shall take our rightful place in this world.'

Theo turned and looked at Calista and mouthed, 'Is she talking about me?' Calista had just enough time to nod before Arachne continued.

'The Mistress will arrive in one hour, and using the power granted by her all-powerful master, the one who began it all, we shall strike at Chiron and his people. And this time, we will leave no survivors.'

'We've heard enough. I think it's time for us to get out of here,' Theo whispered.

Calista nodded, and grabbed Theo's arm.

At first he thought something was wrong, then his head swam and his stomach lurched. He recognised the sensations straight away. She'd done it again. She'd teleported them out of there. Theo closed his eyes and tried not to be sick.

'Intruder!' bellowed a voice.

'It's okay, Oracle it's us,' Theo said, turning around to face the temple table.

First he felt the wind, then the warm sunlight. Then he realised the voice wasn't Oracle's. They were back in the cave opening, high above the sheer drop, and two armed arachne warriors were guarding the entrance.

Theo activated the Sword of Chronos and sliced through the end of the spear as the first guard thrust it at him.

'A little warning next time you do that,' he said to Calista, as the guard backed away and drew a sword.

'Sorry,' Calista said, shrugging her shoulders. 'I

didn't want to risk Arachne and her gang seeing the light from your portal so I brought us here.'

The second arachne charged in. Theo blocked the incoming spear, spun round and slapped the flat of his blade against his naked, human back. His cry of pain and frustration echoed around the small space.

'Do you trust me?' Calista asked.

'I think so,' Theo said, blocking the first arachne's sword blow.

'That will have to do. Take my hand and hold tight.'

As soon as he took hold of it, she ran past the two startled arachne, pulling Theo behind her.

And jumped straight off the cliff edge.

CHAPTER TWENTY-FOUR

'I don't trust you that muuuuuuuccccch!' Theo screamed as they shot out into the air and began to fall.

'Turn into the arachne again. Now!' Calista screamed.

'No. I never use the same trick twice,' Theo said, watching the ground rush closer and closer.

'Theo, we're going to—'

'Now it's your turn to trust me,' Theo said, arching the Sword of Chronos through the air before them. A portal opened. A split second later, Theo fell through it, dragging Calista behind him.

Theo wasn't sure which hurt the most, his shoulder slamming into the floor of the Hall of Heroes, or Calista landing on top of him.

'You weigh more than you look,' Theo said, rolling clear.

'Charming!'

'My goodness,' said a startled Oracle.

'What are you playing at, boy?' Pappou barked as he stepped away from the table and held out his hand to help Calista up. She ignored the gesture and got up by herself.

'Escaping Arachne and her army. There's no time to waste with explanations. We've important news,' Theo said.

'You were lucky you were holding her hand. You know the portal closes after you pass through it.'

'I know,' Theo said.

'See? This is why she's dangerous. She's encouraging you to do reckless stunts.'

'I am not,' Calista said, putting her hands on her hips.

Theo looked at her. It *was* her idea to jump, but there was no way he could tell Pappou that.

'Perhaps he was showing off the—' Pappou continued.

'I hate to interrupt,' Oracle said, 'but I believe Kyrios ton Pithon said something about important news.'

'Oracle,' Calista said, putting her hands on the edge of the temple table and leaning on it. 'Access the sword's memory core and replay what happened in the cave.'

'Memory core? What are you talking about?' Pappou said, standing alongside her and looking disapprovingly at her hands. As if to mock him further she began drumming her fingers on the smooth, cold surface. Theo nudged her.

Calista stopped and turned to face Pappou. 'The Sword of Chronos remembers everything that happens around it over a twenty-four hour period and stores it inside its handle. Didn't you know that?'

'Well...of course I did, it's just...' Pappou blustered. 'Oracle, did you know?'

'Of course, Ninety-Eight, but you have never requested the function and I have never needed to suggest it as an option before.'

Calista folded her arms, a satisfied smile on her face. 'Don't feel bad, Xever. When you've lived a hundred lives like me, it's amazing the knowledge you acquire.'

'I have downloaded the memory core,' Oracle announced.

'Oracle, please play it,' Theo said, standing between Pappou and Calista.

The Hall was suddenly awash with the familiar blue light.

'Let me show you something else,' Calista said, putting her finger back on the edge of the table and moving it to the right. The hologram flickered as she fast-forwarded through the recording, past Theo falling off the edge, making their way through the passage and into the cave, and finally to travelling back one hundred and eighty years.

'How did you know how to do that?' Pappou

asked. This time his voice seemed more resigned, perhaps even impressed.

'Once upon a time the Guardians *worked* with me,' Calista answered.

'Right,' Theo said, cutting in before Pappou could say anything. 'This is what you need to see. Play it from here, please, Calista.'

'Of course, Theo,' she said, smiling at Pappou.

The three of them stood and watched what had happened in the cave.

'This is terrible. She's going to use their own children against them. We need to warn Chiron,' Pappou said. 'Now.'

'I agree,' Theo said. 'But what about this boy she refers to. Do you think she means me?'

'I'm not going to lie to you, Theo, it's extremely likely,' Pappou said heading for the chest where Theseus's old clothes were kept. He threw it open and knelt before it. A few seconds later he stood up with a sword in his hand.

'And the mistress she mentions?' Theo asked, dreading the answer.

'Medea?' Pappou suggested.

'But she was dragged away into gods knows where last summer by whoever she was serving,' Calista said. 'And he didn't sound happy that she'd ruined his plan.'

Pappou nodded. 'Whomever her master is, he's obviously given her another chance. You must be careful, Theo. This time it will be personal.'

'Yes, Pappou.'

'No stunts. No showing off.'

'Yes, Pappou,' Theo said, looking at Calista.

'Don't I get a weapon?' she asked, pointing at the sword in the old man's hand.

'No,' Pappou answered.

'Why? Because I'm a girl?'

'No, because I don't have any to give you. But more importantly, I still don't trust you.'

'Even after what Theo and I just found out? Even after I just showed you how you use your own equipment more effectively?'

'Theo,' Pappou said, ignoring Calista's questions, 'get us to Chiron's camp. They said there was an hour before their mistress arrived, but they might have brought it forward now they know we've discovered their plan. No matter what happens, let me deal with Chiron. You two got off to a bad start, but hopefully, he still trusts me. Trust is *very* important.' Pappou shot Calista a look.

Theo sighed and said. 'You need to stop this.'

'Stop what?'

'You know what. Calista's here to help, and she's done an excellent job so...'

'So? What are you trying to say, Theo?' Pappou said, staring at his grandson.

'Don't make me pull rank on you,' Theo said, standing up as tall as he could. 'Is that clear, Ninety-Eight?'

Theo thought he saw a flash of hurt in Pappou's

eyes, before his grandfather turned away and said, 'Let's just get on with it.'

Theo opened his mouth to say something, to apologise, but then he decided he had no need to. Pappou was being rude and he was just sticking up for his friend. And besides, he *was* in charge, he was the Kyrios ton Pithon.

'Ready?' Theo said to Calista. She nodded, her face red. Had he embarrassed her? Had he embarrassed himself? Pushing his thoughts to one side, he activated the Sword of Chronos and created a portal.

As soon as they stepped through, the three of them were surrounded by centaur guards, their lances or bows aimed at them. Klopian stepped closer to them.

'It's good to see you've increased your security, my friend,' Pappou said.

'Quiet, human. You were told never to return,' Klopian said.

'Please don't be like that, my friend, we've known each other since you were a foal,' Pappou said.

'Because of the friendship we once had, I'll give you the chance to surrender your weapons, as a show of good faith.'

Pappou threw his sword onto the ground and looked across at Theo. 'Do it, Kyrios ton Pithon. We don't have the time to waste.'

Theo couldn't look at his grandfather, it felt strange him calling him by his title, but he left the blade attached to the hilt and threw the god-weapon down. Klopian stepped forward, went down on his front knees and picked them up.

'Move,' the centaur ordered, and, surrounded by guards, they were led through the village. Everywhere Theo looked, centaurs stared back at him. He could see the hatred in their eyes. And he couldn't blame them. The place felt dead without the sounds of children laughing and playing.

When they arrived at Chiron's house, Klopian knocked on the door. Theo thought he heard the leader of centaurs respond and then Klopian opened the door.

Chiron stood in the middle of the room, his lip curled into a sneer for a moment and then he reared up on his hind legs so high that his head almost touched the ceiling.

'How dare you return unannounced, Xever. And bring more humans with you,' he said, looking at Calista.

'Lord Chiron—' Pappou began.

Theo put his hand on his grandfather's forearm and smiled at him. Pappou nodded at him, his face full of love and pride once again. They both knew this was Theo's time, his moment to put things right. Theo stepped forward and dropped to his knee, head bowed before the mighty centaur.

'Lord Chiron, I come with an apology. And grave news. I apologise for our sudden arrival, but there wasn't time to arrange an audience.'

'You think this display will convince me to forgive

you?' Chiron said, waving his hand dismissively. 'That I will lift my curse?'

'No, merely that you will listen to what I have to say.'

'I will listen, but make it brief. Any trickery or pleading, and I will have you all ejected from here. I assume you have completed your task and found where our children are?'

'We have, but I have bad news. News so terrible we must prepare, in more ways than one.'

'We? *We* will not be doing anything together. Once you have delivered your message you can go back to whatever hole you crawled out of. And, if I am satisfied, I may lift the curse. But, if you ever return…'

'My Lord, I know you are angry, but you must listen. The arachne are about to attack again. And this time they will not take any prisoners.'

'We will not allow them to. We will kill their army before they have the chance,' declared Chiron proudly.

'But, My Lord, their army, they will return...they will return with...'

'Spit it out, boy. If you are to be believed, there is no time to waste.'

'They are returning with your missing children. For while only a handful of days have passed for you, for your children, it has been twenty years.'

'What?'

'They have been living in the past and have been brought up by Arachne to hate you.'

'What nonsense is this?' Chiron said, a fresh sneer on his lips.

'It is true, My Lord,' said Calista, stepping forward and bowing. 'I have seen it, too.'

'And who are you?'

'Do you not recognise me, Lord Chiron?' Calista asked.

'No. Should I?' he replied, gruffly.

Calista rose and stepped past Theo. 'Look into my eyes, and what do you see?' she said, rising up on to her tiptoes so she was a little closer to his line of sight.

At first Chiron screwed up his eyes, no doubt expecting some trick, then they went wide.

'Is it really you?' he asked, his voice full of shock and wonder.

Calista nodded.

'It must be you. You have young eyes, but I see the soul of someone who has lived one hundred generations.'

'All right, don't rub it in, Chiron,' Calista said.

The old centaur smiled. 'It is you, isn't it? No one else would dare speak to me like that.'

'It is I, Ariadne.'

'When will this force arrive?' Chiron said. 'Boy, I am talking to you, now.'

Theo looked up, startled by the centaur's sudden change of attitude. Was there nothing Calista couldn't do? 'At any time, My Lord.'

'Then we must prepare. Boy, get to your feet and

prove to me you really are Kyrios ton Pithon. Ariadne, get on my back,' Chiron said.

Theo rose to his feet and watched open-mouthed as Calista mounted Chiron in one swift movement. The centaur walked over to the wall where his weapons were mounted.

'I assume you want the bow,' he said to Calista, taking the lance off the wall.

'Artemis would be disappointed if I didn't.' Calista smiled.

'What?' said Theo, 'Are you saying Artemis taught you archery?'

'I did say I knew her, and that she was a great teacher. Or weren't you paying attention?' Calista said.

'They were good days,' Chiron said. 'Klopian, return their weapons. It is time to carry out the plan.'

CHAPTER TWENTY-FIVE

Theo thought the centaur village would silently wait in hiding, but as they made their way to the communal area, Chiron explained his plan was exactly the opposite.

'We knew they would be back, or someone else would,' he said. 'Last time they took us by surprise, but this time we will be ready. And it will be them that are taken by surprise.'

When they got to the centre of the village, the centaurs were busy preparing for an evening around the fire — tuning musical instruments, placing food and drink on the tables. Everything they did looked natural, making Theo wonder if in fact they were preparing at all. None of them even had weapons.

'This table is for you. I've had chairs brought out for you. Hide your weapons and don't, I repeat, don't, drink the liquid in the jars,' Chiron said, pointing at two ceramic pots in the centre of the table. 'You may stay on my back, Calista, but you must hide the bow for our trap to work.'

Theo looked at the chair he'd been supplied with. It was tall like a bar stool. It had to be because the table was so higher than normal to suit the height of the centaurs.

Although everyone was talking and doing their best to look normal, Theo could feel the tension. The centaurs seemed to be holding their breath, fighting the urge to survey the trees that bordered the village.

Chiron, on the other hand, looked prepared and confident. Perhaps that was just what a leader did, even when he knew the fate of a village and its people rested on his shoulders.

'Everyone knows what to do, I'm sorry there's no time to explain. Just wait for the signal,' Chiron said. 'We just have to trust in each other.'

There was a faint smile on his lips as he said the words, but Theo couldn't fail to notice that the centaur still refused to look at him.

Chiron walked off, and talked to a nearby centaur, Calista looking very proud of herself on his back.

Theo and Pappou climbed up onto their chairs and listened to a group of centaurs who started playing musical instruments. Soon all the villagers began singing. The bonfire was lit and the warmth and gentle music began to make Theo feel sleepy.

He was sure he felt his eyelids dropping when he something caught his attention — a bright red flash — in the dark forest on the hillside.

'Pappou? Did you see that?' he said, resisting the temptation of looking in the direction of the flash.

'See what?'

Before Theo could tell him, more red flashes appeared. The first few up on the sides of the valley, their brilliance partially masked by the leaves and undergrowth. But then the sharp bursts of light grew closer until they were appearing in the pathways between the buildings that circled the gathering of centaurs and humans.

The arachne had arrived, swords or bows in hand. And they had surrounded the square.

There was an eerie moment of silence and then all Tartarus broke loose. The nearest arachne began shooting webs from their spinnerets or firing arrows at the nearest targets. The centaurs screamed and took cover behind their tables.

Theo shifted on his seat, his fingers touching the hilt of the Sword of Chronos as two arachne appeared around the corner of the building nearest them. Threads of silk flew out of them and latched onto the centaurs sitting at the table next to them, dragging them to the ground.

Theo jumped down from his chair and reached into his pocket.

'Wait, Theo. I know we don't know the specifics of the plan, but we must trust Chiron and wait for his signal,' Pappou said, raising his voice just loud enough to be heard over the chaos.

Theo reluctantly nodded as two more centaurs

were taken down, silk wrapping around their legs and binding them together. They were the lucky ones. Some centaurs had arrows lodged into them, writhing on the floor in agony.

'This is all too easy,' the nearest arachne called, his voice filled with laughter and excitement.

'What are we waiting for?' Theo said, reaching into his pocket again.

Then the horn sounded. It was so loud it made Theo jump. That had to be the signal.

All at once, the screams of horror from the centaurs became deeper, terror-inspiring battle cries. The centaurs turned from frightened victims to determined warriors. Weapons appeared as if from nowhere as they reached under the tables and grabbed them from their hiding places.

Theo summoned the power of the heroes and jumped towards the arachne that had been laughing moments before. As he flew towards it, the creature pulled on his bow and prepared to fire, a look of triumph on his face.

The look on the arachne's face changed to fear as Theo willed the Medallion of Morpheus into action. Arms shaking, the beast fired its bow. The arrow flew off wildly and missed as Theo landed on the ground, with a deafening boom.

He had changed into Polyphemus.

The arachne remained rooted to the spot as the battle raged around it. Theo took advantage of the creature's crippling fear and grabbed it around its human torso. It's eight legs kicked wildly as he lifted it into the air.

'You should not have come back,' Theo roared in his face before throwing the terrified arachne into another that was running to his aid. The pair rolled across the floor in a tangle of spider legs and human arms.

Theo took a step towards them, but three non-warrior centaurs pounced on them. They began tying the arachne's legs together with rope but were forced to duck and dodge as webbing flew out of the arachne's spinnerets. One of the centaurs was too slow and a line of silk wrapped around her body, pinning her arms to her side.

Theo was about to help free her, when another centaur ran to the nearest table and picked up one of the jars Theo had been told not to drink from. She threw its contents over her trapped friend. The spider silk began to smoke and then turned brittle and crumbled into dust.

Satisfied the centaurs were safe, Theo looked for his next target.

To his left, Chiron charged through the enemy, his lance striking an unsuspecting arachne in the abdomen, sending it tumbling into the wall of a nearby house. Calista was still on his back, firing arrows at the enemy as she went. Every arrow she fired hit its target as she laughed and ducked incoming arachne arrows or spider threads.

Theo was about to find another enemy to attack

when he felt something hit his left hand, followed by both his legs and his neck. A violent tug tore at his ankles and before he could try to resist it, he was pulled from his feet. He hit the ground, crushing two tables under his huge cyclops shoulders.

While he'd been surveying the battlefield, four arachne had crept up on him and fired silk at his hulking form. Struggling on the floor, and thankful his right arm was still free, Theo reached into his pocket, withdrew his sword and activated the blade. He looked at his ankles, aimed, and swung the sword down. It cleaved through the air towards the spider silk.

And stopped.

'No!' Theo yelled in his deep cyclops' voice. Another thread had wrapped around his wrist. Now all his limbs were trapped.

You're a giant, remember. Use your strength! Perseus reminded him.

Flexing his huge muscles, Theo pulled on the thread around his sword arm, hoping to snap it, or at least drag the arachne along. But nothing happened.

Theo looked around him, the four arachne had spread out, pulling their silk tight. The thread might be strong — it had stopped him falling from the cliff after all — but he should still be able to pull them closer to him. Unless… Yes, it was the hairs on their legs. They were helping them grip the floor just as the ones on his legs had helped him climb the cliff when he had transformed himself into an arachne.

'Pappou!' Theo yelled as another arachne added a tether to his right arm. They all began to pull and shorten their lines.

'Pappou,' he cried again, but either he was busy or the old man simply didn't hear him over the deafening thunder of battle.

The silk threads tightened around his limbs, digging into his wrists and ankles. They were getting tighter, smaller as the arachne pulled. Sweat poured down Theo's chest and back. He couldn't resist it much longer. More arachne were running in, their weapons raised. Several arrows thudded into his huge, projected body. They had started to injure him and once it got too much the projection would disappear and he would revert to his normal self.

And then it came to him.

His normal self was smaller. And if he was smaller…

The idea flashed through Theo's mind and commanded the medallion to stop its magic. Losing the projection around him, Theo dropped to the ground, landing flat on his back.

The gathered arachne hissed and prepared to fire or descend on him with their swords, but Theo didn't hang around. He kicked his legs free of their bindings and scrambled back to his feet.

Drawing once again on the hero's energy, he ran at the nearest arachne. Several of the others fired at him and he cartwheeled one-handed, the arrows and spider silk missing him as he spun round. Once he was back on two feet he continued running and flipped over the first arachne's head, his sword connecting with hers. As soon as he landed behind her, and out of the circle of oncoming arachne, he ran.

You are getting better at this. You are coming up with your own plans and solutions, Perseus said. *But, why are you running? You could have defeated them.*

I need to find Pappou, Theo thought back as he ran towards the bonfire, searching through the melee of arachne and centaurs. The warriors fought off the invaders while the civilians threw jars of the dissolving liquid over anyone who was trapped. The centaurs were winning. All around him, arachne lay tied up on the floor. None of them looked injured. It was then that he noticed something was missing.

'Where are the children?' Theo said, talking to the heroes.

Maybe they changed the plan after you discovered it. No time to worry about it now, they're following you, Perseus warned.

Theo looked back over his shoulder, and sure enough the six arachne who had trapped him were coming. He ran at the nearest house, pumping his arms furiously. He jumped and ran *up* the wall, the heroes lending him their strength, speed and power. When he got near the roof he pushed off, flying away from the wall, over the top of four of the pursuing arachne.

Stunned, the arachne watched as he arched over the top of them, sliced the sword down and opened a portal. As he landed on the ground, he brought the blade down hard onto the earth, bending and shaping the portal so it covered them like a parachute. The arachne had just enough time to look into the crackling, black abyss before being sucked inside.

Theo deactivated the portal just as the last two arachne caught up. He brought the sword up, ready to defend himself, but the spiders stopped and began to back away.

'Afraid, are you?' Theo said.

'No,' the thing hissed. 'It is time for the mistress to begin phase two of the plan. This is where the tide turns. Let's see how your friends like fighting their own.'

Red flashes sparked down streets and alleys.

Theo looked on in horror as he realized what the arachne meant.

The kidnapped children had finally arrived.

CHAPTER TWENTY-SIX

Theo watched in horror as red lights flashed in front of him and two fully-grown centaurs appeared. They looked fearsome. Armour hung down the sides of their hairy bodies, and gleaming chest plates and helmets protected their human half. Each were equipped with swords that were drawn and ready to use. Theo had just enough time to see the hatred that burned in their eyes before they ran off and began attacking their own kind.

Theo couldn't help it, he stared as twelve of kidnapped centaurs began to fight the villagers — their parents, aunts and friends. The villagers desperately defended themselves, while trying to beg the children to stop.

'No!' Chiron shouted, charging through the ring of houses opposite Theo and back towards the bonfire. Calista desperately clung onto his human waist. 'We must *all* stop this, now! You don't know what you're doing!'

To Theo's surprise, the armoured centaurs stopped attacking. The villagers backed away and lowered their weapons. Had Chiron's commanding presence brought the attacking centaurs to their senses?

'Whatever you say, old man. You're the one we want,' one of the young centaurs shouted. Then all twelve of them charged towards Chiron, their legs galloping at incredible speed, barging past the centaurs that had put their weapons down.

Theo knew Chiron would not fight them. He had to get to the centaur leader before they did, and somehow stop them. There were about twenty metres away, but at the speed they were travelling at, and with their head start, he had no hope of outrunning the young centaurs.

He looked at the sword in his hand and then at Calista. What would she do?

Saying the chant in his head, brought down the sword and ran through the portal he cast in front of him. He stepped out the other side, appearing right in front of the old centaur and his rider.

'Kyrios ton Pithon, do not attack them,' Chiron rumbled. 'They know not what they do.'

'I don't intend to,' Theo said, looking over his shoulder. Calista, who had two arrows nocked, lowered her bow.

The kidnapped centaurs continued to charge. They would be upon them in seconds.

Over the sound of their thundering hooves, Theo heard the deep clatter of wood at his feet. He looked down. Chiron had thrown down his lance.

Theo took a deep breath and deactivated his blade. He didn't drop it. He couldn't risk being completely unable to defend himself and the others.

'If it's revenge you want, take it,' Chiron said to the charging centaurs in a calm, powerful voice. 'But know this. Arachne has deceived you in the worse possible way. I don't know what she's told you, but you are our family, our children, and I would die first rather than harm any of you.'

The kidnapped centaur at the front of the charging dozen put his hand up and they all came to a halt a few metres from their intended target.

'Harm us? You abandoned us,' the one who appeared to be in charge called.

'That's not true,' Chiron answered steadily.

'Arachne told us the truth. When we were born, you ordered that we be left outside the God Shield, because there were already too many mouths to feed. Luckily for us, we were found by our Mistress and she gave us to Arachne.'

'She is lying to you. You were taken from us, just two days ago.'

'Ha!' the centaur said. 'Arachne told us you would say that.'

'What Chiron says is true,' called a female villager. She walked closer, putting the empty jar of web dissolver she had in her hand on the only table that was still standing. Tears gathered in the corners of her eyes. 'Hepion, you are my son. I would never abandon you. You were stolen from me.'

'Quiet!' the kidnapped centaur snapped.

'You must listen, Hepion, please,' she said, her tears finally released. 'You have grown so much, even though you have only been gone a handful of days, but I can still tell it's you. Look, you have the same markings as me.' The mother pointed down at the hair on her legs.

The young centaur stepped closer and looked at the woman's legs. 'They do look the same, but that proves nothing except that we are related. It doesn't mean you didn't abandon us to die.'

'Please,' the mother said, weeping. 'You must listen to us. You have been lied to your whole life. Here, I have something for you.' The female centaur reached into a satchel she had over her shoulder and pulled something out.

Theo peered closer. It was a soft toy in the shape of a centaur.

'It is yours. I gave it to you on your birthday, the day before you were taken.'

Tentatively, the centaur stepped closer. He reached out for the gift and then pulled his hand back. 'Why would our mistress lie to us?'

'A good question,' Chiron said, 'with a simple answer. She wants to hurt *us*. Punish *us*. By taking you and feeding you lies for the last twenty years, she'd hoped to get the perfect revenge. She's turned you into weapons, but you are only tools in her plan. She does not care about you. If you fight us now, hurt your own mother, your own father, then she has achieved all that she set out to do. Then she will tell you the truth of how she kidnapped you and you will realise what you have done.'

Hepion raised his sword. 'Enough talk. You are defenceless. We could take our revenge on you alone, Chiron, just as you alone took the decision to leave us to die.'

'You must do what you think is right,' Chiron said. Then he did something that took Theo by surprise. He got down on his knees and bowed his head.

'Old fool,' Hepion said, flexing the grip on his sword as he looked at Chiron's neck.

Theo felt his throat go dry as the angry centaur stepped closer, raising his sword higher. 'Wait!' Theo cried, rushing forward and causing all the other kidnapped centaurs to go on alert. 'What if we can prove what Chiron is saying is true?'

'Quiet human,' Hepion sneered, thrusting his sword towards Theo, before turning his attention back to Chiron. 'Look at you. You allow a human to ride on your back. You allow a human to defend you. Have you no self-respect?'

'Quite the opposite,' Chiron replied. 'I respect all life, all races.'

'Really?' Hepion said, looking at the captured arachne.

'They attacked us. We had no choice but to defend

ourselves. Klopion?' Chiron called to his lieutenant. 'How many arachne causalities have there been?'

'There have been none, just as you ordered. They have only been captured and bound.'

Theo squirmed. He'd sent some to The Net. He hoped he hadn't ruined whatever plan Chiron had been acting out.

'In that case, you won't mind if we cut the arachne free. Men,' Hepion ordered the other kidnapped centaurs.

'Wait, Hepion,' Theo said. 'I know you think the arachne are your allies, but they're not. If you free them, they will turn on you. I can prove that Chiron is telling the truth and that you were stolen from these good people as babies. Please, just let me. Give me this one chance. Give your mother this one chance.'

Hepion turned and looked back at the rest of his warriors, then at his mother, who still held out the cuddly toy. He was thinking about it, Theo could tell. Maybe Hepion's resolve was weakening.

'Very well,' the young leader said. 'But make it quick.'

'Calista, I need your help. We need to show the recording of—' Theo stopped when he saw her shaking her head.

'I'm sorry, Theo. The sword can't store information from that long ago.'

'You are just wasting our time,' Hepion said.

'No, wait,' Theo said, hearing the desperation in

his own voice. 'I have another idea, but I need to use this sword to help me. Don't be afraid.'

'I am *not* afraid!' Hepion sneered.

Theo panicked at his ill-chosen words. He was about to apologise but decided it was best to keep his mouth shut. Nodding, he stepped away from Chiron and the lost children so that he had plenty of space and his actions wouldn't be seen as an attack. He also needed Hepion to be able to see up the cliff behind Chiron.

Saying the chant in his head, Theo brought the sword down. The rip appeared, the usual crackle of energy skirting around the edges, leaping and dancing as the portal widened. The gathered centaurs moved away, regardless of which side of the battle they were on.

'Theo, you can't go through. You can't enter your own timeline,' Calista warned.

Theo smiled up at her. 'I'm not going to, I just want them to see.'

Calista nodded encouragingly. She must have guessed what he was going to do.

Theo deactivated his blade and moved to the side of the opening. 'Come closer, Hepion, and see the truth. Come all of you.'

At first Hepion didn't move, then he peered through the opening. 'What is this?' he asked, his curiosity dragging him closer to the portal.

'A gateway to the past. Similar to the way Arachne transported you here. Look through it and see her lies,' Theo said, slowly moving closer to the armoured centaur so they could look together.

Through the portal they saw the centaurs and arachne fighting in the events that passed two days ago.

'See, we are enemies. This proves nothing,' Hepion said, thrusting his weapon forward.

'Keep watching,' Theo replied, his voice calm and even. He knew Hepion would soon see the truth.

The armoured centaur took a step back as an arachne flashed past the portal. 'What's that, on its back?' Hepion asked as another arachne went past carrying a silk wrapped bundle.

Hepion moved even closer and bent his human half forward so that his nose was almost touching the portal. Behind him, Theo heard the others moving too, drawn in by Hepion's curiosity as well as their own.

'What can you see?' one called.

'I…I see the arachne attacking centaurs and… and…stealing their children. Stealing…us. It's true,' Hepion said, shaking his head as he stepped back, his hooves making barely a sound.

'How can you tell it's you, my son?' Hepion's mother said, taking his hand in hers.

'Some of the silk bundles,' Hepion said, swallowing. 'They have legs or arms poking out. Sometimes both. Our arms and legs. Sumolus,' he said, turning to one of the other centaurs, 'I recognised your birthmark, just as my mother recognised my markings.'

'This happened two days ago,' Theo said, watching Hepion squeeze his mother's hand.

'Mother. I...' he said. Dropping his sword, he threw his arms around her.

Theo felt his body flood with emotion — relief, love, and even a little sadness — as he thought about his own mother.

The air was filled with the clatter of weapons as the other centaurs dropped them and the two opposing sides came together.

'Sumolus,' a male centaur cried. 'It is I, your father.' The two slowly moved towards each other and then everyone started calling out names and rushing forward.

'Take these arachne and lock them up,' Chiron said to one of his lieutenants.

'Not so fast, Chiron, Kyrios ton Pithon. This isn't over yet,' came a fresh voice.

Theo felt his blood freeze. He recognised the voice straight away. He turned towards the direction it came from.

A woman was standing on the roof of one of the centaur homes. She was wearing the black leather outfit he had seen her in the last time they met. The cape, made from the skin of harpy wings, flapped gently in the wind behind her. She had no visible weapons at her side.

'Medea,' Theo said. 'Why am I not surprised? You always have to make an entrance.'

'How disappointing,' she said, looking down at

the communal area. 'I was hoping you would say something about how I was supposed to be dead.'

'I'm not foolish enough to think that. So, you *are* the mysterious mistress we've been hearing about. Hardly a surprise. Your plan has failed. We beat the arachne and proved to the centaurs you were lying to them.'

Medea laughed. 'I haven't lost, boy. The war has only just begun.' She lifted her hand for everyone to see and snapped her fingers.

For a moment Theo thought she was going to use some kind of magic, but it only a signal.

A signal that would change everything.

'You said I like to make dramatic entrances. I think you might be right,' Medea said as she stepped to one side. Two arachne joined her.

Suspended between them was Pappou.

CHAPTER TWENTY-SEVEN

'Let him go!' Theo barely managed to say through his tight throat.

'Keep back, young one,' Medea said, pointing a finger at him, a spark of red energy dancing around its tip.

Theo felt the warmth of someone's hand wrap around his. It was Calista. She had climbed down from Chiron and joined him.

'You know, boy, you are a most tiresome individual, who brings me nothing but trouble,' Medea said as she brought her hand up to her face and inspected it. The red spark multiplied and soon more than were possible to count swirled around her upraised hand.

'Let my grandfather go,' Theo shouted at her.

Medea shook her head. 'Why couldn't you just play along and act the way you were supposed to?'

'I don't understand.'

'No, you don't. And that's the problem. Perhaps with a little more encouragement...'

'What kind of encouragement?' Theo said, knowing it wouldn't be good. 'Let my grandfather go and I'll listen to what you have to say.'

Medea shook her head and rubbed her hands together, spreading the crackling red light to both her hands.

'Theo, be careful. She's up to something. That energy,' Calista said, 'I'd recognise it anywhere. It's the time energy that held me and Theseus captive in her hideout last summer.'

Medea stepped forward, brought her hands in front of her face, and moved them out so that her body formed a cross.

'Guards,' she said over her shoulder, 'release him.' The arachne let go of Pappou, dropping him to the floor like he was nothing more than a bag of rubbish.

Theo went to step forward, but Calista held him back.

Chiron came and stood on his other side, lance in hand. 'We must work as a team if we are to defeat her,' he whispered.

'Fear not, Chiron,' Medea said, somehow overhearing his words. 'My work here is almost done. I'll let you keep your children — for now. But mine...' Medea flicked her hands forward and the crackling energy flew off her fingers and took on a life of its own. It flew through the air like shooting stars, striking the captured arachne and her two guards, making them disappear.

'You are unwise to leave yourself unprotected, Medea,' Chiron called.

'I am completely safe. You will not order your troops to shoot your arrows at me. You are too...*good*,' Medea answered, saying the last word like it was something disgusting.

Chiron snapped his fingers and all around him the centaurs turned their bows on her, including the ones she had kidnapped.

'After what you have done to our children? Our families? My warriors are crack shots. They don't have to kill you, but they can disable you and you will face justice for what you have done.'

'You are forgetting something. My arachne slaves might be gone, but I still have your friend, Xever.'

Theo watched helplessly as Medea raised her hand. Forks of red lightning sprung from her fingers and down towards Pappou. His body rose from the ground, his arms limp, his head drooped, the lightning looking like the strings on a puppet.

'My power has grown considerably since we last met, Kyrios ton Pithon. Here, let me show you.'

Pappou's body began to shake violently and a cry escaped his lips.

Theo gripped his sword, took a step forward and stopped. He wanted to act but he was afraid. If he acted, he could save Pappou. But it might also give

Medea an excuse to do something…something terrible.

'Fire!' Chiron ordered from behind him.

Theo heard the arrows take flight and rush over his head towards their target.

Medea gave a terrible laugh. Energy streaked from her fingers, striking the incoming arrows. Every single one exploded.

'Too late, Kyrios ton Pithon,' she said, unleashing another surge of power through Pappou's body.

'Leave him alone,' Theo cried.

'Come and stop me, boy!'

Theo summoned all the hero's energy. He ran and jumped so that it almost looked like he was flying toward the roof. He landed on the tiles and brought his sword up, ready to strike. Before he could, Medea used her strings of energy to throw Pappou at him. His grandfather's limp body slammed into him, knocking him down.

'Pappou!' Theo cried as his grandfather's body rolled over the edge of the roof and disappeared.

'Pathetic,' Medea snapped.

Theo leapt to his feet and raised the sword again.

'You shouldn't have given Pappou back. You've nothing left to bargain with. You've just lost.'

'Maybe you should check on your dear, sweet grandfather first. Until next time, boy,' she said, snapping her fingers. She vanished in a spitting crackle of red energy, her mocking laugh the only clue she was ever there.

'Pappou?' Theo cried, running to the edge and looking down.

'It's all right, Theo. I have him,' Chiron said. Pappou was cradled in his arms.

Theo jumped down from the house as Chiron placed Pappou on the ground.

'Quick, get a medic,' the centaur leader ordered.

'Pappou,' Theo said, throwing himself down onto the ground beside his grandfather.

'Theo, I'm...sorry,' Pappou said breathlessly.

'Try not to talk. Save your energy,' Theo said, tears flooding his eyes. 'You've nothing to be sorry for. It'll be okay.'

'I can feel Hades calling to me. I've had a great life, Theo. Don't be sad. My only regret is that I won't see you become the adult, the hero, I know you'll become.'

'Don't talk like that. You're not going to die. You can't leave me,' Theo said, desperately trying to hold himself together.

Pappou smiled. 'It's my time. I am tired and ready to see the gods. I also want to see your grandmother again. I've missed her. And you, you are more than ready to take my place.'

'No. We can get you to a hospital. I can go back in time and...'

'No!' Pappou said with such force he descended into a coughing fit. 'Promise me you will not do what you're thinking. The dangers are too great. If you do, you might save me, but The Net...The Net. You must protect The Net.'

Theo felt someone touch his shoulder. It was Calista.

'Calista, promise me you will do everything you can to stop him if he tries,' Pappou said, reaching out and taking her other hand.

'Yes,' Calista answered simply.

'But...' Theo weakly protested.

'Theo, I am proud to have you as my grandson. When I see your dad, I'll tell him how proud he should be, too. Theo, tell your mother that...that I am proud of her t—'

Pappou's eyes flickered closed and his head rolled gently to the side.

The whole village went silent for a moment and then Theo threw his head back and screamed. Grabbing his grandfather's body, he pulled him close. 'No! No! Hades? Zeus?' Theo shouted, looking up at the sky. 'Don't do this. Don't...'

'Theo…' Calista began.

'This is my fault. My fault. It was because I tried to stop her.'

'No. You can't blame yourself, Theo. Come on, we need to let the centaurs sort this out for you,' Calista said, moving in front of him so he could see her.

Theo turned and glared at Chiron. He had ordered the arrows to be fired. He had placed the curse. No, if there was anyone to blame, it was him. Theo started to get up and noticed all the gathered centaurs. They all looked shocked and upset. Chiron was crying. He hadn't even cried when the children had been taken.

Theo let his anger go and held Pappou for a few more moments. He gently lowered his grandfather onto the floor, took hold of Calista's hand and rose on his jelly-like legs.

First Dad, then Gran, and now Pappou.

'Why does everyone have to die?' he asked, looking at Calista through tear-filled eyes. She didn't answer, she just put her arms around him and let him cry.

CHAPTER TWENTY-EIGHT

Theo stepped through the portal and threw his bag and the Sword of Chronos onto his bed. He'd been away with the centaurs for almost a week. Slowly, he began to work his way through his grief. Chiron had avoided him for days, until, under the encouragement of Calista, Theo had gone to him and explained he didn't blame him, or the curse, for Pappou's death.

'I am relieved you have come to this decision,' Chiron had said. 'The truth is, I removed the curse the morning after I placed it upon you. I realised that I had been...over-zealous. The people needed to see I was going to do something, and I allowed myself to be pressured into something I knew wasn't right. I was afraid you would not believe me after the tragedy that has befallen you.'

Theo stayed for a few more days, making plans with Chiron and Calista until he had no choice but to return home. He could not put off the inevitable any longer. After much soul-searching, Theo concluded that there was only one way to tell Mum about her father's death, and that was to explain everything.

The only thing was, Pappou had chosen him to be his successor instead of his daughter for a reason. She was exceptionally rational, and only believed in things you could see, hear and touch. Even if she would find the truth hard to accept, there was no way Theo was going to pretend Pappou had died in his sleep. His grandfather was a hero and his story deserved to be told.

The alarm clock next to Theo's bed went off and he reached out and pressed the button to mute it. Then he heard his mum's through the wall. He always set his to wake him up one minute before hers.

She was up straight away, he could hear her moving around. If she followed her usual routine (and she always did) she would go into the shower in her en-suite bathroom. She would be twenty minutes.

With nothing else to do but worry, Theo plugged in his phone. The battery had died days ago.

Theo heard his Mum leave the shower. He shook his head as if to awaken himself from a dream. He had been staring at his wall the whole time.

Glancing at his phone, he noticed it had enough charge to start up. He turned it on. The screen lit up and the familiar blue light began to flash. It was a message from Mia. Theo was about to ignore it, when he changed his mind. It was something to distract him while he waited to tell Mum.

Still having dreams. This time I dreamt you were in danger. Are you all right? Still, with that sword you can change anything bad about your life. You're so lucky.

Theo put the phone down and didn't answer her. He had more important things to do. Instead he went downstairs, feeling numb, like a robot. The stairs seemed to go on forever as he made his way down them.

His plan was to make breakfast, sit Mum down at the table and tell her over a cup of tea. That's what people did at times like this.

He put the kettle on and sat at the breakfast bar.

'I thought I heard you come down,' Mum said as she came into the kitchen, her hair all bundled up on top of her head and wrapped in a towel.

'Cup of—' Theo started to say, following his plan, but the words caught in his throat and stayed there.

'Theo, are you all right?' Mum said, narrowing her eyes.

'No,' he managed to say before he ran across the room and threw himself at her. A few seconds later he felt her arms wrap around him and pat his back tentatively.

'What's wrong?'

'It's Pappou,' he said, all his plans about what to say and do forgotten.

'What about him?'

Mum started to push Theo away, but he held on, tightening his grip. 'He's...he's dead.'

'Don't be daft, Theo. You've just had a bad dream.'

'No. I was there,' Theo got out before taking a sobbing lungful of breath.

'You're not making any sense, Theo. Pappou's hundreds of miles away. You've had a nightmare, that's all.'

'I wish...I wish it was,' he said, his whole body shaking.

'It's ten o'clock there. He probably hasn't gone out for his daily swim yet. I'll call him.'

Theo wanted to tell her he wouldn't answer, but his throat was raw. Besides, she wouldn't believe him. He let her go and allowed her to walk away and pick up the phone by the fridge. He watched her press the memory dial for her father and then he looked at the floor, his head hung low as he wiped away his tears.

The phone rang and rang.

'He's probably already left. We'll try again in an hour before Gran and Granddad arrive to look after you for the day. If he doesn't answer, just give him a call every hour. I'll tell Gran it's all right to make the international calls.'

'You're not listening to me — as usual,' Theo said, his grief suddenly turning into anger. 'He's dead! I let her kill him.'

'Theo, you need to calm down,' Mum said, putting the phone down. 'Why don't I make you a nice cup of tea?'

'I don't want a cup of tea. I want Pappou back. And Dad.'

'Is that what this is all about? Theo, you've clearly got a lot on your mind. Your brain must be all muddled up after our argument and turned it into a dream.'

Theo stopped and took a deep breath. This was going as bad as he had expected. Worse maybe. He had to find a way to get her to listen.

'Mum, please, believe me. This is so hard. Pappou's gone. The centaurs have him.'

'Centaurs? Now I know you're hysterical. You've even got Pappou's stories mixed up in your dreams.'

'It's not a dream. The centaurs are real.'

'Theo, these creatures you're talking about, they're just stories.'

'That's what I thought too, and then Pappou showed me they were real.'

'Real? His imagination is even wilder than yours,' Mum laughed, but Theo thought he heard a crack in it.

'Please, Mum. Don't. You'll feel terrible when I show you the truth.'

'Show me?'

'Yes,' Theo said, wiping away his tears. 'You need to come with me, to the centaur village.'

'Oh, I give up,' Mum said, throwing her arms up

in the air. 'Gran can deal with you when she arrives. Obviously, you won't listen to me anymore. Perhaps you should go back up to your room and come back down when you're ready.'

'Fine!' Theo said. He ran upstairs and slammed his bedroom door. Tears streaming down his face, he realised he only had one choice. There was no way he would ever convince her. He had planned on telling her, and then taking her back to the centaur village. Perhaps he would just have to throw her into the deep-end, shock her into accepting the truth.

Unplugging his phone, Theo shoved it in his pocket, and grabbed his pack. Once it was on, he gripped the sword with both hands and brought it down through the air opening a portal in front of his bedroom door.

Wiping the last of his tears away, Theo opened the door a fraction and called to his mum. 'I'm sorry, Mum. Can you come up here, please. I need to talk to you.'

Theo waited for the sounds of her footsteps as she came up the stairs.

'Mum!' he called. He felt bad about what he was about to do, but there was no other choice.

'I'm coming,' she called, her tone betraying her feelings. She was getting cross. She thought he was being silly. Well, she wouldn't think that in a minute.

The door opened and before she could stop herself, Mum stepped through the portal.

CHAPTER TWENTY-NINE

Theo followed his mother, deactivated the blade of the Sword of Chronos and stuffed the hilt into his pocket.

They were in the middle of the communal area of the centaur village. In place of the usual bonfire was a flat, rectangular one that ws waiting to be lit.

'W-where are we?' Mum asked, her mouth open, her head turning from side to side as she took in everything around her.

'Allow me to introduce myself.'

Mum whirled around at the sound of the voice.

'Dr Harpe, my name is Chiron. It is with great sadness that I welcome you to our home.'

'Chiron?' Mum turned and faced Theo. 'Is this a joke? Some friend you've dressed up?'

'Elizabeth — may I call you Elizabeth? — this is no costume and I am afraid this is no joke.'

'Theo...' Mum began. Her lips continued moving

even though no sounds came out. For the first time Theo could remember, Mum was lost for words as she gazed around her, seeing the gathered centaurs, the houses, and the sea of brightly coloured flowers that decorated the area in front of the fire.

'I tried to explain, Mum, but…' Theo said.

'Elizabeth, with your permission we would like to begin the ceremony,' Chiron said, his voice soft.

'Ceremony?' Mum said, removing the towel from her head which had been there since she had got out of the shower.

'To celebrate the life of our dear friend, your father, Xever Harpe.'

'Celebrate the life…' Mum stopped and looked at Theo.

'Yes,' said Chiron.

'You mean…' Mum said as she continued to look at her surroundings, the irrefutable proof all around her.

'Yes, Mum. This is Pappou's funeral,' Theo said, freeing the tears which had gathered in his eyes.

'I don't believe you,' Mum said, although Theo could hear the doubt in her voice. 'I want to see my father. I need...'

'Of course,' Chiron said. 'Theo, you know where to go.'

'Mum?' Theo said, taking her hand.

Together they walked away from the flat bonfire and through the rings of buildings. The centaurs they passed bowed respectfully. Wherever Theo looked, he saw faces etched with sadness and devastation. The whole way, Mum's head turned left and right and back over her shoulder as she stumbled along, taking it all in.

'This is all real, isn't it?' Mum asked.

'Yes. It is,' Theo answered her.

They stopped outside Chiron's house.

'He really is...gone, isn't he?'

Theo bit his lip in an effort to keep his tears in and nodded.

'Dad's inside?'

Theo didn't answer — couldn't answer. He opened the door and led his mother inside. Light poured down from the ceiling, illuminating the middle of the huge, round room. Raised up on a beautifully carved table, surrounded by flowers, lay Xever Harpe.

'I'll leave you alone with Pappou,' Theo said. 'I've already said my goodbyes.'

'No. Please stay,' Mum said, bending over and kissing Theo on the top of his head. Theo nodded and together they walked forward in silent tears.

The sun slipped behind the mountains that formed the Pelion Peninsula and the sky rapidly turned from pale blue to a much darker shade. Theo looked up at the stars as they slowly appeared, one-by-one.

'Are you all right?' Mum asked from his side.

Theo nodded, unwilling to speak in case he started

to cry again. Calista stood on his other side. She looked solemn and not at all like herself. Theo wasn't sure if he liked it that she was being respectful or if he would prefer her to be her usual, cheeky self.

The whole of the centaur village had gathered in the communal area, young and old. The flat fire was in front of them with a clear path leading up to it.

From somewhere in the distance, a horn sounded and everyone in the congregation stood to attention. Theo felt his mum take hold of his hand and he leaned against her.

A moment later, Theo heard the sound of marching hooves. The beat grew louder and louder until Theo thought he felt the ground shaking beneath his feet. He glanced to the side and saw Chiron marching down the aisle. He was bringing his knees up high. In his hand he held his battle lance. It pointed straight up. Tied onto it, half way down, was a piece of fabric like a flag flying at half-mast.

Behind him came four more centaurs carrying Pappou between them. He was suspended on wooden poles that went across their backs, his body hidden in a sea of flowers. Four more centaurs followed behind.

The funeral party stopped in front of the unlit fire and the four centaurs at the back moved next to the ones carrying Pappou and, taking hold of the wooden poles, they lifted him up, carried him forward and put him on top of the stack of wood.

Theo stared up at Pappou. He didn't notice the

eight centaurs leave. A tear slipped from his eye. Mum pulled him closer.

'Xever Harpe, or Pappou as his grandson called him, was a friend to the centaur people, a servant to the gods of Olympus and a hero to all who live on Earth, even if they didn't know him or what he did,' Chiron said.

Theo wanted to look at the wise, old centaur, but couldn't bring himself to do it.

'He was a kind, determined man, and the best friend anyone could ask for. I remember the first time I met Xever. He was...'

Theo stopped listening. His mind was filled with his own memories. He shut his eyes, let the tears fall and his shoulders shake, as he remembered the good times.

The times he would never have again.

He wasn't sure how long he'd stood like that, his body pressed tight against his mother's, when he felt her move. He opened his eyes. A centaur was stood in front of him with a flaming torch in his hand. He moved it towards Theo, who seeing his mother already had one, took it from the centaur's hand.

'And now we must say our final farewell to our friend as we send him on his way to Charon, complete with his coins to guarantee safe passage across the river Styx,' Chiron said, a flaming torch gripped in his hand.

'Come on,' Mum said, leading Theo to the stack of

wood. They stood next to Chiron. The old centaur looked at them and gave them a sad smile.

'Ready?' he said.

Theo nodded and the three of them moved their torches closer to the huge pile of wood and set it alight. Chiron bowed. Theo copied and moved back into his place as the heat from the fire grew and grew.

The flames spread through the wood and all the gathered centaurs moved away, not from the heat but to form a huge ring around fire at the very edge of the communal area.

'Theo, Dr Harpe,' Calista said, 'Please, follow me.'

Calista led them to a space in the circle next to a table. She reached up and took a bow and arrow that were waiting on it and passed it to Theo.

'There's one for you, too,' Calista said handing another to Mum before collecting one for herself.

'What do I do with his?' Mum asked.

'Just copy everyone else,' Calista said.

Chiron lifted his lance up into the air and cried, 'Beware, Hades, a warrior is coming!'

'A warrior is coming!' the gathered centaurs repeated and pulled back on their bows, pointing them up in the air.

Theo brought his bow up.

'I wish I'd known him better,' he heard Calista say, and then everyone released their arrows into the night sky.

CHAPTER THIRTY

The rest of the night went by in a bit of a blur. Food was eaten, glasses were drained and the centaurs took it in turns to tell stories about Xever Harpe, their friend and hero. Some were sad, some had a lesson to be learned, but most were funny. Many mentioned his Hawaiian shirts.

Finally, tired, and confused by the party atmosphere, Theo made his way back to Chiron's house, where he and his mother were staying for the night. He had no idea where Chiron was staying. No doubt any number of centaurs would offer up their home to him.

Theo climbed into bed and was about to slip into what he hoped would be a dreamless sleep when his phone went *ping*. It could only be from one person — Mia.

I hope you've had a good day. Feel like you're

ignoring me. Let me know if I can help you with anything. Time travel sounds like fun.

Theo wished he hadn't read it. He put the phone on silent under the bed so it wouldn't disturb him again, rolled over, faced the wall and closed his eyes, hoping to fall asleep.

But it was too late. Mia's message had started his brain ticking.

If Pappou hadn't expressly told him not to, Theo knew he would risk it all, to first save him and then save his dad.

Frustrated and alone, Theo eventually fell asleep.

Theo awoke the next morning. His eyes stung and he had a terrible headache. Even though he couldn't remember them, he knew he'd had bad dreams because his pillow was on the floor and his sheets were wrapped around him.

'Morning,' Mum said, looking around the corner of the wall. She was doing her best to look brave and happy. It didn't fool Theo for a moment.

'Morning. How did you know I was up?'

'I've been stood here for a while, just watching you. I used to do it all the time when you were younger. Sorry if it's weird.'

Ordinarily, Theo would have told her it was, but

today he shook his head. Today it seemed like the most wonderful thing a parent could do.

'I stayed up late last night with Chiron and your friend Calista. They've...they've explained a few things to me. After breakfast, I want you to take me to the Hall of Heroes. Did I get the name right?'

Theo nodded.

'We need to continue Pappou's work. You have to continue *your* work.'

'Mum…' Theo began, but he didn't really know what to say.

'Let's eat, and then you can show me where you and Pappou have been hiding all this time. I never did believe his story about how you broke your rib last summer — or his staircase.'

Theo smiled and knew that even though Dad and Pappou were gone, everything would be all right.

'Is that a model of Olympus?' Mum said, rushing into the Hall of Heroes, unable to contain her curiosity.

'You're good,' Theo said, quickly following after her as he deactivated the Sword of Chronos. 'I thought it was the Parthenon the first time I saw it.' Theo expected her to start explaining why it couldn't have been, but she didn't.

'And these must be the vases you told me about.' Again, she dashed over and crouched so she could get a better view of the paintings. 'If these were in a museum they'd be worth a fortune. How did they end up here?'

'I'll tell you later,' Theo said, remembering his diving adventure last summer. 'I need to introduce you to—'

'Welcome, Kyrios ton Pithon and Ninety-Nine. I wish I could find the words to console you and explain how I am feeling.'

'Who said that?' Mum cried, rotating on the spot, looking for the mysterious woman who had spoken.

'It's okay, Mum. That was Oracle.'

'Oracle? As in the Pythia, the Oracle of Delphi?'

'That is exactly who I am, Ninety-Nine,' the disembodied voice answered.

'You sound like a computer. Is that why you can't explain how you are feeling?'

'Mum!' Theo said in horror.

'I am *not* a computer, though I suppose both your father *and* your son use me like one. I...I will miss Xever.'

Theo smiled sadly, noticing Oracle's use of his grandfather's name.

'I have a complete record of everything your father did and achieved during his time as a Guardian of The Net. Much of it I can play in the form of holograms.'

'Some other time,' Mum said, stepping back over to the table and taking one of the books out of the column shelves. 'This is fascinating. *You* are fascinating. So, Pythia, how do you work?'

'Interesting that you ask,' Oracle said. 'Your father

was never interested, or many of the other members of the Bloodline of Theseus for that matter.'

'"That it works is all that matters to me",' Theo said, repeating what Pappou had said to him about the mirrors a year ago.

'I suppose Pappou was gently eased into this by his father, my Pappou, Mum said. 'I...I've had this somewhat forced upon me.'

Theo put his hand on his mother's shoulder.

'This is in Ancient Greek,' Mum said, opening the book.

'You can read it?' Oracle said, the surprise clear in her voice.

'I can read a number of ancient languages. I've even translated the Rosetta stone and the Dead Sea Scrolls. Hang on,' Mum said, tapping her finger on the page in the book. 'This signature…it says Plato.'

'Yes, it does. Are you familiar with the great philosopher?'

'Am I? I've read all of his works, but never this one,' Mum said, carefully turning the book over, looking for a title. 'Do you have some gloves I can wear?'

'You will not have read this one. It is the only copy and was written especially for one of our earliest Guardians. It deals with the concepts—'

'If you don't mind, I'd like to read it for myself.'

'Of course, Ninety-Nine. Gloves are not required. The Hall protects it, as it protects us all.'

'I know. I can feel it,' Mum said. 'It's like I belong here. I feel…'

'Calm?' Theo said.

'Exactly.'

'If I may, you are not acting very calm, Ninety-Nine,' said Oracle. Theo had the same thought. Mum was acting like a kid in a sweet shop, but he wasn't going to complain.

'Oracle, please, call me Elizabeth,' Mum said.

'Of course, Ninety-Nine.'

Theo chuckled, remembering Pappou's constant battle with Oracle to get her to call him by his name.

'So, Oracle, tell me everything I need to know,' Mum said, turning to face Theo, her eyes alight with passion and excitement.

'I am afraid I have already told you *too* much. I have let my excitement get the better of me and now that I have come to my senses I shall tell you no more,' Oracle said.

'What do you mean?' said Mum.

Theo knew exactly what Oracle meant. 'I'm afraid you need to be initiated,' he said.

Mum closed the book. 'I don't know if I like the sound of that.'

'Don't worry,' said Theo, a wicked smile spreading across his lips. 'It only hurts a little bit.'

Mum slid the book back on the shelf, took a deep breath and turned back to Theo. 'What do I need to do?'

'We will need the sword, Kyrios ton Pithon,' Oracle said.

'Not a problem,' Theo said, tugging the hilt out of his pocket and extending the blade. 'Right, Mum, hold it like this, and get ready to show off your knowledge of ancient Greek.'

As soon as the initiation was complete, Elizabeth Harpe began asking Oracle question after question after question. Theo didn't think he'd heard either of them any happier.

Theo felt his phone vibrate in his pocket and then heard a *ping*. He took it out and read the message.

Theo are you ignoring me or are you off having an adventure. I had a dream. Your grandfather died. It felt so real. Not the one I met the other day. The other one who lives in Turkey. Hope you're okay and not travelling through time so you can save him.

Theo stared at the message. How could she be having dreams about him and his grandfather? She'd had the others because they were blocked memories that were resurfacing, but this...

Ping!

It was another message from Mia.

'Excuse me, Kyrios ton Pithon, but what is that irritating noise?' Oracle said.

'Just a text message,' Theo said, holding up the phone for Oracle to see, even though she had no physical form.

'But that is not possible.'

'What do you mean?' Theo said, knitting his eyebrows together.

'If you remember, The Hall of Heroes is not within our normal plane of existence.'

'I know. We're one second behind the rest of the world. But that's okay, the message will just arrive one second later.'

'That is not quite how it works. For all intents and purposes, we do not exist in your world. The mobile phone signal cannot find us, it is impossible.'

'Then how can Mia send me messages?'

'Mia? Who's Mia?' Mum asked.

'The girl I met on the holiday camp,' Theo answered, as he opened the pictures folder on his phone and started to flick through them.

'Is that the girl you had round the other day?' Mum said.

'Yes,' Theo said, showing Mum a photo on his phone.

'Theo,' Mum said, shaking her head. 'Whoever that is, she isn't a girl.'

Theo took another look at the photo. Had he had shown her a picture of Amanda by accident? No. It was definitely Mia. 'Of course she's a girl.'

'No, she isn't. She looks older than me.'

Theo stared at the picture. It seemed to flicker for a moment as if there was another image beneath it.

'Kyrios ton Pithon, please bring your mobile device to the table,' Oracle said.

'What's happening?' Theo asked, as he put the phone down on the red fabric.

A beam of blue light came down from the temple roof and scanned the phone. 'We have a problem,' Oracle said.

'Why? What is it? What can you all see that I can't?'

'Ninety-Nine is right. That is *not* a girl.'

'Then who is it?'

'One moment, Kyrios ton Pithon. I am carrying out a brain scan that should negate the effects of the medallion.'

'The Medallion of Morpheus?' Theo asked.

'No, but I suspect Mia, whoever she really is, has been using one, or something similar. I have located the memory in your brain. Please hold your phone while I sterilise the area.'

'Sterilise? Oracle, what do you mean, sterilise?' Theo said, his voice rising in panic.

'Do not worry. This should not hurt.'

'Wait! Wait,' Theo shouted.

'Yes, wait,' said Mum. 'I want to know more about this sterilisation before—'

'It is done,' Oracle announced.

Theo was about to ask what was supposed to happen, when the image on his phone screen changed.

He was no longer looking at Mia. He was looking at a woman with black hair. Anger and fear rose in Theo in equal measure. He was looking at the woman who had killed his grandfather.

He was looking at Medea.

CHAPTER THIRTY-ONE

'But, that's impossible,' Theo said, staring down at the photo of Medea.

'Of course it is not,' Oracle said. 'You do it, and we are discovering the medallion has new abilities all the time.'

'Are you suggesting she has an amulet like mine?' Theo's hand went up to his chest and felt the piece of bronze through his clothes. 'Wait!' he cried, suddenly realising. 'Of course, she wears that big, clunky bracelet! That must be it.'

'It is possible. It might also give us some clue as to who Medea's mysterious master is,' Oracle said.

'What do you mean?'

'The amulet — all the artefacts you possess — was created by the gods. Inside, it harnesses the very raw power of the gods. Not only that, each artefact contains god energy in order to power it, just like your mobile phone has a battery. No mortal can create them. It is impossible. You have no energy sources that can deliver enough power.'

'So, this master must be a god,' Mum chipped in.

'Exactly, Ninety-Nine.'

'Or someone powerful enough to control a god's energy,' suggested Theo.

'It is unlikely that is the case.'

'Wait,' Theo blurted. 'I just thought of something.'

'What is it?' asked Mum.

'When Mia, or should I say Medea, came to our house, I told her about the artefacts, I even offered her the chance to hold them. She didn't want to, which I thought was strange after all the fuss she'd made. I wonder...when I confronted her before, she touched my golden fleece belt and was thrown across the room. Maybe the same would happen again if she touched the artefacts.'

'That particular incident was due to the build-up of temporal energy,' Oracle said, 'but it is possible the artefact she was using to disguise herself could interact with any of yours, and it might not have ended well. I hypothesise that the energy within your artefacts may be the opposite of the energy used in hers.'

'Like good and evil. Or the lights that are produced when portals are opened.'

'Exactly. Or the poles of a magnet.'

'So, we know she managed to fool me, but how have her messages been able to penetrate the God Shield at the centaur camp as well as here?'

'That is an excellent question,' Oracle said. 'Please place the phone back on the table and I will scan it more thoroughly and see what I can find.'

'Perhaps I can help,' Mum said.

'Thank you, Ninety-Nine. I would appreciate that.'

Theo looked down at his screen and deleted the photo of Medea. He couldn't bear to look at it any longer. He couldn't believe he'd been so easily tricked. He placed the phone on the table and stepped back while Oracle did her thing.

Mum and Oracle's voices seemed to muffle as Theo thought back over the last few days. What was Medea up to? Her false friendship couldn't have been about acquiring the artefacts because she was unwilling to touch them. What was it she was after?

'Kyrios ton Pithon, we have found something.'

Theo looked over. Mum's face was a curious mixture of dread and the satisfaction of having discovered something.

'What is it, Oracle?' Theo said, stepping towards the table.

'It is bad. Very, very bad.'

Oracle never sounded happy and cheerful, but with that one sentence, she sounded as if she had discovered the end of everything.

And perhaps it was, Theo thought. Pappou was gone and... He took a deep breath. He would have to deal with that later.

'What is it?'

'Your mobile device has several viruses on it,'

Oracle began. 'One is vastly different from the others and I do not believe it is mortal-made. This virus has taken on a physical form and become a separate circuit within your phone.'

'It's become hardware,' Mum added. Theo couldn't tell if she was frustrated at Oracle's long-winded ways or as a scientist just wanted to join in.

'This piece of hardware has fused itself onto your phone's circuit board, hiding in the background, not damaging it, but living off it like a parasite.'

'Like a leech sucks blood from a victim, or a flea on a cat,' Mum said, looking at Theo.

'Yes,' Oracle agreed. 'But unlike a leech, it is not feeding off the phone.'

'No, it doesn't need to,' Mum said in awe. 'It has its own power source.'

Theo looked at his mum. She was staring at him as if she was waiting for him to say something.

'Is this power, god energy?' he asked.

There was a long pause before Oracle answered, 'Yes, it is.'

'So how did this...' Theo paused while he thought of a name for what was on his phone. 'How did this godware get onto my phone?'

'Good question,' said Oracle. 'There are no energy signatures that suggest teleportation.'

'You mentioned viruses. Could it have been sent in an email or a text mess—' Theo abruptly stopped. He knew. He knew how she did it.

'What is it, Theo?' Mum asked.

'That's it,' he said, stepping away from the table. He began to pace back and forth as everything fell into place.

'Theo, what's wrong?' Mum asked.

He walked towards the chest. 'It's the messages. All of this. Medea's plan has been all about the messages. She must have installed the godware when we swapped numbers. But that was only the start of the plan.'

'What do you mean?'

Theo felt a tear roll down his cheek and he quickly rubbed it away. 'Nearly all of her messages have been about Dad and using the sword to change the past.'

'I see,' said Oracle.

'What?' asked Mum.

'She wanted Theo to create another paradox. One so large it would exhaust all the god's power and bring down the Net,' said Oracle.

'And I resisted. I refused to take the bait and so...and so...' Theo couldn't say the words. He collapsed onto the chest and put his head into his hands.

Theo didn't hear his mum walk over, but felt her sit next to him and put her arm around him.

'You can't blame yourself for what happened to Pappou,' she said gently.

'Then who do I blame?'

'Medea and her master. They made this happen. You were doing the right thing. You did what Pappou would have wanted you to do. He would have rather died than see the monsters unleashed on the world.'

Theo turned and looked at his mum. She was crying too.

'He was stubborn like that,' Mum added.

'Is that where you get it from?' Theo said, managing a smile.

'Yes, and right now we have job a to do. We have to honour Pappou and his memory. And we have to stop Medea from getting whatever she's after. She's getting desperate. We need to be careful.'

'Kyrios ton Pithon? Ninety-Nine? I have discovered something else,' Oracle announced.

Mum leant forward, kissed Theo on the forehead and stood up. 'What is it, Oracle?'

'There is a signal emanating from the phone. We have been exposed. The enemy knows where we are.'

Theo leapt to his feet. 'That is *not* good.'

'On the plus side, I may be able to use it to find out their position.'

'Get working on it. Will we need to evacuate? Can you leave the Hall, Oracle?'

'The vases can certainly be removed. I...I am not sure about myself.'

'Xever was right. These are indeed dark times,' said a deep voice from behind them.

Theo turned and looked at the figure in the tunnel entrance. He knew instantly that it was not an intruder. He had spoken to him twice but had never seen him in his physical form before. It was the king of the gods. Calista stood beside him, her bow and arrow ready.

Zeus was an imposing figure. Tall and muscled, his thick, white beard almost concealing his mouth. His eyes were wrinkled and kind.

'You really need to get some heating in here,' he said, wrapping his white robes around himself.

'We must leave, My Lord. We have been discovered,' Oracle said.

'I know, Oracle.'

'Of course, you do,' she said.

'That is why I am here. The Pantheon's powers are low, but I have used what little remains to come here and do what must be done. It will leave Olympus with just enough power to survive, but if the enemy get in here all will be lost and so—'

Before Zeus could finish what he was saying, the Hall of Heroes was filled with red light, blinding Theo for a moment. Then he heard the familiar skittering sound of the arachne moving across the floor and walls.

'Intruder. Intruder. Intruder,' Oracle blared.

Theo activated his sword and stood in front of his mother.

Calista drew her bow and prepared to find a target.

Zeus roared, his voice drowning out all the other sounds in the enclosed space, and threw lightning bolts at the nearest enemy.

'We're too late. They're here,' he boomed. 'Theo,

Calista and I will protect your mother. Go! Go to Medea, but if anything should go wrong, I will not be able to help you.'

Theo barely had time to turn and look at his mum before everything around him flashed with white lighting and his body went limp.

CHAPTER THIRTY-TWO

Theo woke up to discover he wasn't in the Hall anymore. He was lying on the floor in a rectangular tunnel. Unlike the natural, smooth surfaces of the tunnel into the Hall, these walls were tiled. The roof above him had a slight curve to it. Most importantly, instead of the usual green-blue illumination from the torches, the light ahead was red.

Then Theo felt it. The slight sense of unease. The opposite sensation his mother had felt when she arrived in the Hall of Heroes.

Had Zeus teleported him to the Hall of...Villains?

'Mum?' he whispered, peering into the half-light around him. He called again, but no answer came.

Thankful that he hadn't dropped the Sword of Chronos when he collapsed, Theo walked towards the light, dodging the puddles formed from the water dripping from the ceiling.

As he stepped into the crimson area, a deep, coarse voice cried, 'Intruder. Intruder. Intruder!'

Theo ignored it and took in the area in front of him. It was like a twisted version of the Hall of Heroes. The walls were covered in dark tiles, but unlike the smooth, straight tunnel he had just walked up, they jutted out at sharp angles as if someone had tried to turn their bathroom into a something that resembled a cave. Just like the Hall, torches lined the walls, their red flames flickering. In the centre of the room was the Hall of Villain's version of the Olympus table.

Dark and twisted, the table was made from black stone. The corners rose up in the shape of four tall, spire-like mountains. Flames flickered out of the top of each one.

Somehow, Theo knew he had seen what it represented before. It was a replica of the dark place where he had fought the minotaur when it had teleported him away from Pappou's house last summer.

'Theo?' came a quiet voice. 'Thank goodness, you've found me.' Mia popped out from the far end of the table, her hair a mess, her clothes covered in dirt. 'You must help me. These huge monsters with the body of a spider and—'

'Forget it,' Theo snapped. 'I know who you really are, *Medea*. I should have guessed days ago. Mia. Medea. It hardly takes a genius to work it out.'

Mia tipped her head to one side and then a smile

covered her face. 'What does that say about you, then, boy?'

'It says that I'm trusting, open and honest, and expect others to be the same.'

'That's *your* problem,' Mia replied, her face changing, revealing her true identity. When she spoke again, Mia's youthful, cheeky tones were replaced with Medea's cold, callous voice. 'You know, it's those same pitiful qualities that caused your grandfather's death.'

Theo clenched his teeth and gripped the Sword of Chronos.

'It's been fun using this little toy,' Medea said, raising her wrist and exposing her favourite bracelet. 'I guess I no longer have a need for it. I've achieved what I set out to do.' She removed the piece of jewellery and threw it onto the black table as she walked around it.

'No, you haven't. What you really wanted was for me to cause a time paradox so that it would bring down The Net and you could dominate humankind, just like you tried before. But just like before, I've beaten you.'

'True,' Medea said, the smile disappearing from her face. 'But while my plan has not been a complete success, the Hall of Heroes is now destroyed. Yes, Theo, the heroes will not be lending you their support this time. The vases are destroyed and without them their spirits are useless. Who knows what has happened to that know-all Oracle.' Medea paused, smiled and added, 'Or your mother.'

'I trust, remember?' Theo said boldly. 'And I trust Zeus to have saved them all. My Mum isn't helpless either, she's clever and—'

'You *are* naive. Zeus is no hero, he's petty and cruel. Have you learned nothing from the stories your grandfather told you? Sorry, my mistake. Your *dead* grandfather.'

'I...' Theo began, but her comment stabbed into the very soul of him.

'Now, we see the truth. Without your toys, the voices in your head, and your *friends*,' she said the last word like it was something unclean and disgusting, 'you are nothing. You are just a frightened little boy. You are on your own, but I... Well, I have a whole army of arachne at my disposal and something else.'

Theo stared at her but didn't respond. He wasn't going to give her the pleasure of asking her what it was she had.

'He's very angry,' she continued, 'and he wants a rematch. Don't you, Minie?'

Theo heard the familiar clip, clop of the minotaur's hooves. He turned and saw it come out of the darkness behind him. The huge beast stopped, its head bowed so its horns would miss the ceiling. Theo turned back to Medea, confident that her pet would not attack him until she ordered it to.

'I have somewhere to be,' Medea said. 'Don't worry, I will be back, but until I return, why don't you two get reacquainted.'

Before Theo had a chance to respond, she clicked

her fingers and disappeared in a dazzling burst of red, sparkling light.

Theo spun round to face the beast. With no heroes to guide him, he had to think fast. And if he didn't have them, he would have to use the other advantages he had.

Let's see how he likes fighting himself, Theo thought, feeling himself rise up off the floor as the minotaur raced towards him.

The minotaur didn't seem bothered by Theo's sudden change into another of its kind. It swung its fist, hitting the projection the Medallion had created around him squarely in the ribs. Theo staggered back from the force of the blow and heard something clatter onto the floor.

He stared at his empty hand. The sword. He'd dropped the sword!

The minotaur came at him and unleashed another punch. Theo brought his arm up and blocked the attack. Not knowing what else to do, he threw himself at the minotaur, wrapping his arms around the beast's wide, hairy chest. They staggered and spun round before crashing into the black stone table. A sharp *crack* filled the air as their combined weight broke it. They fell through the middle of it, Theo landing on top of the minotaur.

Theo scrambled off the beast and stared at it. The minotaur wasn't moving. Had he killed it? Shocked, he deactivated his disguise, but before he could try and find the Sword of Chronos, the room filled with a bright flash of red.

'I'm back,' Medea said. 'And I've brought another friend.

Theo spun round. She was with a man.

They moved closer, into the light.

The man was in motorcycle leathers.

Theo's eyes widened as a word caught in his throat.

The word was *Dad*.

CHAPTER THIRTY-THREE

'What's going on? Where am I?' Theo's father said, glancing around the room, his eyes lingering on the fallen minotaur. 'What on earth is *that*?'

Before Theo could answer, a violent pain stabbed through his head. He stumbled and fell to his knees, his hands clasped over his ears as a cry burst from his lips.

'Are you all right?' the man said, rushing forward.

'No,' Theo cried, his voice strangled by the intensity of the throbbing in his head. Then, as suddenly as it started, the pain disappeared. Images flashed though his mind, confused, disordered and contradictory. Just like with Akanthus, Theo now had two sets of memories.

The first were of when his father had died on his motorcycle. But in the new set, Dad had walked out of his grandfather's house saying he was going out for a ride. But his motorbike was left in the bright Cypriot sun on the drive. Mum had called the police and reported a missing person, but his father had never been found. He had disappeared without a trace.

'Dad? Is it really you?' Theo said, getting back to his feet.

The man shook his head sadly. 'Sorry, you have me mistaken for somebody else. I do have a son, but he's only eight. Look, I don't like the look of this place, let's—'

'It's me, Dad. I'm twelve now,' Theo said, staggering forward over the ruins of the table. 'And I've missed you so much.'

'I...' The man began and then stopped. Theo could feel his father's eyes staring intently into his and then... 'Theo?'

'Yes. Yes, it's me.'

Theo clambered over the last piece of wreckage. He reached forward, his fingertips just millimetres away from his father's hand.

And stopped.

His eyes snapped to Medea. She had slunk back into a shadowy corner and was barely visible.

Theo slowly withdrew his hand.

'What are you up to, Medea?' Theo asked, stepping away from his father.

'I'm simply giving you what you want,' she answered from her darkened corner.

'I know what you're up to. This isn't about what I

want. It's about what you want. Your plan didn't work, so now you're—'

'Theo, we've got to get out of here,' Dad said, reaching out to grab his hand.

'Dad, don't—'

Theo felt the warmth of his father's hand for an instant. It was gentle but strong. Love and kindness flooded into him and then...

Crack!

Theo was thrown across the room, his body unconscious before he hit the tiled wall.

'Yes. Look at it. Look at the chaos!'

Theo's head rolled to one side as Medea's jubilant cries woke him from his unconsciousness. She stood over the remains of the shattered table watching a fragmented hologram that somehow was still functioning. The minotaur was gone.

Worst of all, there was no sign of Dad.

A groan escaped Theo's lips as he pushed back to his feet. Attracted to the sound, Medea turned to look at him.

'Good,' she said triumphantly, 'you're awake. Come and see what you've done. Know that this time your world truly belongs to my master. You see, boy, we have been playing the long game, my master and I, and while you resisted even the allure of having your father back, *he* could not resist *you*.' She stopped to laugh before adding, 'Your world has been undone by a father's love.'

Theo stood at Medea's side and watched the images. The missing minotaur was climbing up the London Eye. Theo could see the terrified faces of the people inside the capsule as the beast hammered on the glass with his huge, hairy fists, his hot breath fogging the glass and covering it with saliva.

'There's more. Look. America,' Medea said with a wave of her hand.

With a burst of red light the image changed. Arachne were charging down the streets of New York, jumping on cars, tipping over busses and climbing up the huge posters and gigantic TV screens that covered the buildings. People ran screaming everywhere.

'Do you want to see some more?' Medea asked. 'You should see what they're doing to the Acropolis.'

Theo shook his head, he only had one thing on his mind. 'What have you done to my dad?'

'I wish I could tell you, but he could be anywhere. You know, Theo,' she said, 'it was you who gave me the idea after you did it to Minie last time. It took us months to find my little pet. He was just floating about, lost in time, not really alive.'

Theo made a fist and fought down the anger bubbling up inside him.

'And without your precious gods to help you, there's nothing you can do about it. Any of it. Even *if* Zeus somehow found the power to recreate The Net and put all of my master's creations back in it, he wouldn't have the power to make the world forget what they have seen. I'm afraid life as you know it is all over.' Medea stopped and looked at Theo, an expression of sympathy on her face. 'You know, your dad is probably the lucky one. And Pappou. At least they won't be enslaved.'

Theo stepped away, his legs weak, as her words echoed around inside his head. 'I...I hate you,' he spat.

'Good. That's exactly what I wanted,' Medea smiled and turned back to watch the horrors displayed in the hologram.

Theo watched her. He couldn't be sure if the light he saw in her eyes was the reflection of the hologram or delight at what she had achieved. One thing was clear, she thought he was broken, defeated and wasn't taking any notice of him.

But he wasn't. Not yet.

He backed away and returned to where he'd been thrown. The Sword of Chronos had to be somewhere. He quickly glanced at Medea to check she was still engrossed in her victory and then began searching. He frantically surveyed the ground, but the weapon was nowhere to be seen. Maybe he had dropped it before he had hit the wall?

Theo turned and checked Medea. She was still engrossed.

He looked one more time for the sword in vain. But he did spot something else. Something bright and shining amidst the black stone.

It was Medea's bracelet.

'I assume you're looking for this,' Medea said, facing him and holding out the Sword of Chronos in her hands. The end of the blade balanced on one hand while the snake tail lay in the palm of the other. It wriggled around so violently that she had to wrap her fingers around it to stop it leaping out of her hands.

'Give it to me,' Theo said.

'Do you think I'm stupid?' Medea said, shaking her head.

'As you've said, there's nothing I can do to stop all this. I just want to see my mum one last time. Let me create a portal and I'll give you back the sword before I go through.'

Medea shook her head. 'That isn't going to happen.'

Theo ran at her, his roar echoing around the enclosed space. Medea brought the sword round and swiped at Theo's head. He dived to the side and landed amongst the rubble of the table. It's sharp edges dug into him and every part of him hurt, but hopefully it would be worth it.

'Pathetic!' Medea hissed. 'You're nothing but a distraction. I'm sure my master will greatly reward me if I finish you and give him this prize,' she said, looking at the sword.

'Don't you ever shut up?' Theo shouted, shifting his position amongst the broken, black stone.

'You're right,' she said, nodding. 'The time for talk is over. It's time to finish this once and for all.'

Theo stared at the length of the blade as she lifted it above her head.

'Time to die, little Guardian.'

Medea brought the sword down.

Theo rolled to the side, revealing the thing he had deliberately covered when he had landed in the rubble.

The sword of Chronos struck Medea's abandoned bracelet. There was a bright, silent explosion. Streaks of green and red energy threw Medea upwards, her body slamming into the roof. The light gathered around her as she remained there, pinned, as it flew around the room, twisting and turning as if it were trying to find a way out.

Theo staggered to his feet and shielded his eyes as he watched the dazzling display. The two colours combined and turned yellow. Suddenly the torrent of energy changed direction and flew towards the tunnel entrance, whipping at Theo's clothes and hair.

With the energy gone, Medea dropped from the ceiling, landing on the floor in front of Theo, her right arm trapped beneath her. She didn't move.

Theo looked down the tunnel where the light had gathered. A figure was standing within it, the yellow light rushing around it like a hundred snakes. The figure raised his hand and the multiple streaks of energy changed whatever direction they were travelling in and instead flew into the up-raised palm.

The Hall of Villains dimmed, the only light coming

from the malfunctioning red hologram. Theo strained his eyes, trying to see who it was.

Was it Medea's master? Had he come to collect her? To finish what she had started?

'We will have to hope it is enough,' the figure said, his deep voice echoing off the walls.

Suddenly the room was plunged into complete darkness.

'Zeus, wait,' Theo called, recognising the voice, but the king of the gods had already gone.

Theo stared around him, desperate to see something, anything, but there was now hardly any light.

He heard a moan and a yellow light appeared.

'My hand. My hand!' Medea cried.

Theo tore his eyes away as soon as he saw it. Her right hand was missing, leaving only a ragged stump with a handful of yellow flashes of energy dancing around the end of it.

'Here, let me help you,' Theo said, moving towards her.

'Get away from me. What have you done?' she cried. Even though she was looking at her ruined hand, Theo knew she was talking about the yellow energy and its disappearance.

Theo allowed himself a gentle smile. 'You told me the gods needed energy to put things right, so I gave it to them. When you tried to kill me, the Sword of Chronos hit your bracelet, releasing both their energies.'

Medea gave a bitter laugh. 'Destroying them both

in the process, you fool. You're trapped here. Trapped.'

Theo fell quiet for a moment as he realised the truth of her words. At least she would be trapped here too.

A sharp *crack* rang out. At first, Theo thought the cave was damaged and collapsing. Then a red, sparking portal opened behind Medea, its entrance growing wider and wider. Theo moved away, remembering what had come out the last time he had seen the exact same thing.

'My master will *always* take care of me,' Medea smiled, getting to her feet and moving towards the portal.

'You have failed me for the second time,' came a deep, cold voice from the portal.

'I...I can do better, Master,' Medea mumbled, clutching her ruined arm.

'We shall see,' The Master replied as a pair of harpies flew through the portal and picked her up.

'You are most welcome to join us, Guardian,' said the unseen voice, the last word said with mocking disdain. 'Zeus has undone all that we have achieved — your world is once again back to normal — but the Guardians are beaten. You have no leader, and there wasn't enough power to rebuild your base of operations. You will not defeat us next time. And there *will* be a next time. Or there would be, if you weren't trapped here forever.' A cold laugh spilled out of the opening and filled the Hall.

'I'd rather die than join you,' Theo called.

'That is likely. Bring her back to me,' said The Master.

Theo stood and watched the harpies fly back through the portal with Medea. It snapped shut and he stumbled back into the dark room. The Master wasn't lying. He was stuck. Without the sword, he would have to remain here.

Forever.

CHAPTER THIRTY-FOUR

Theo sat in the darkness on the hard floor and desperately tried to think of a way out. It was useless without the sword.

'Theseus?' he called, but the only sound that came to him was the dripping water from the tunnel.

Theo pulled his knees into his chest and thought about his mother. Presumably she was safe, but now she had lost him as well as her husband.

Theo felt like crying but then he realised something amazing had happened. Something that gave him hope. Something that gave him a reason to escape this place.

He still had the memories of his dad's disappearance. Was he still alive?

A light swept across the Hall, cutting off Theo's thoughts.

'Thank goodness, you're alive!'

Theo leapt to his feet at the sound of Calista's voice. He ran to her, and threw his arms around her.

'Hey, steady there,' she said, laughing. 'If I drop this torch…'

'You found me.'

'Of course I did. Wherever one of us goes, the other will follow. It's our history and our destiny. I'm only sorry I didn't get here sooner.'

'But how did you get here? Don't tell me you've been *here* before?'

'No,' Calista smiled. 'Oracle managed to get a fix on the location through the signal. Just as she erased your memory, she gave me one just before…'

'Is Oracle all right? Is Mum?'

'Let's go and find out. This place gives me the creeps,' Calista said, as she took hold of his hand.

Theo almost didn't recognise the place now that it was lit up.

'Welcome to our new home,' Chiron said.

Theo peered around the old arachne cave. It looked different now that the centaurs had started to make it their own. They had already constructed the communal area.

'And when I say our, I don't just mean the centaurs',' Chiron said, indicating Theo should look to the right. 'Dr Harpe has already begun to build a new Hall of Heroes.'

Theo smiled. Why was it not a surprise that everyone was calling her that and not Elizabeth? 'Where is Mum?'

'Come, I will take you to her.'

Theo followed Chiron through the busy cave, Calista at his side. All around them, centaurs were constructing their new home.

'Here,' Chiron said, stopping outside a wood and stone building. 'It is the first place we constructed, in honour of your grandfather.'

The door opened. Mum came rushing out and wrapped her arms around Theo.

'Thank the gods you're safe,' she mumbled into his cheek. 'Now,' she said, pushing him away. 'Come and see the new Hall of Heroes.'

'I'd love to,' Theo said, following her in.

Theo stood in the middle of the room, but didn't see anything or hear anything his Mum said. All he could think about was how empty the Hall looked without Pappou.

And about the second set of memories he had of his father.

ACKNOWLEDGMENTS

This story would not have been possible without the considerable help, support and advice from many people. Of those, I would like to send special thanks to Nichola, Claire, The Covert Writers, and Maria.

ABOUT THE AUTHOR

Gareth Baker was a primary school teacher for over twenty years but he decided he'd rather tell stories. Gareth's own childhood left him forever fascinated with heroes and their path of discovery and greatness. This is thanks to such films as *Star Wars* and *The Three Musketeers*. For most of his youth Gareth grew up in the countryside on farms all over England, because his father was a shepherd. Today, Gareth lives in a world of his own, along with his family, with superhero comics, books, films and computer games. He likes to deliberately say words wrong, plays the violin, the ukulele and Singstar. He looks forward to sharing his next book with you soon.

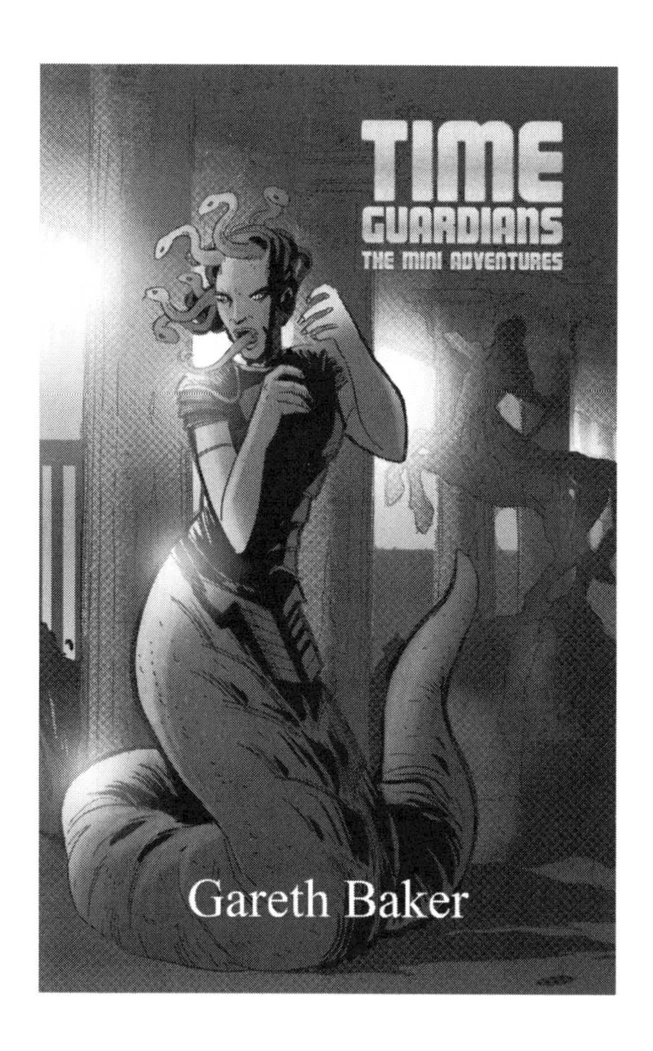

Two exciting mini missions - Theo must face the cetus and the deadly gorgon.

Are you ready for a super-charged adventure into virtual reality?

For more swords and action, follow the adventures of Isomee and Brackenbelly

Find out more at

gareth-baker.com

Videos

Games

Activities

News

Sign up for the newsletter and get all

the latest news

Please try to find some time to

review this book on Amazon.

Thank You

Printed in Great Britain
by Amazon